He W

In his thirty years he [...] woman could pull to attract [...] difference between innocence and calculation. He saw that Penelope had caught him studying her, but she had not looked away. She probably didn't want him to think she was interested. She'd tried to shield herself from him, and could not. She didn't tilt her head and flirt, inviting his interest.

He would have to be careful with her. She was going to take some convincing. How did a man go about it? He wasn't at all sure.

He wondered if Penelope had ever had a man. His rising jealousy was a surprise. He looked at his watch. He'd known her for three hours and twenty-two minutes. How could he be jealous?

It was the season. In the yards, the flowers were blooming. It was spring, and his sap was rising.

Dear Reader:

Welcome! You hold in your hand a Silhouette Desire – your ticket to a whole new world of reading pleasure.

As you might know, we are continuing the *Man of the Month* concept through to May 1991. In the upcoming year look for special men created by some of our most popular authors: Elizabeth Lowell, Annette Broadrick, Diana Palmer, Nancy Martin and Ann Major. We're sure you will find these intrepid males absolutely irresistible!

But Desire is more than the *Man of the Month*. Each and every book is a wonderful love story in which the emotional and sensual go hand-in-hand. A Silhouette Desire can be humorous or serious, but it will always be satisfying.

For more details please write to:

Jane Nicholls
Silhouette Books
PO Box 236
Thornton Road
Croydon
Surrey
CR9 3RU

LASS SMALL

NOT EASY

Silhouette Desire

Originally Published by Silhouette Books
a division of
Harlequin Enterprises Ltd.

*First published in Great Britain in 1990
by Silhouette Books, Eton House, 18-24 Paradise Road,
Richmond, Surrey TW9 1SR*

© Lass Small 1990

Silhouette, Silhouette Desire and Colophon are
Trade Marks of Harlequin Enterprises B.V.

ISBN 0 373 58047 9

22 – 9012

Made and printed in Great Britain

LASS SMALL

finds that living on this planet at this time is a fascinating experience. People are amazing. She thinks that to be a teller of tales of people, places and things is absolutely marvelous.

Other Silhouette Books by Lass Small

Silhouette Desire

To John and Ruth Ranalletta,
who are "family" without being related.
And especially to Ruth,
who inadvertently gave me the idea for this story.

One

While waiting in the police station of Byford, Indiana, Penelope Rutherford watched the people. There was some pedestrian traffic passing her bench in the hall, and there were those who paused as they exchanged words. Since she had been allotted this unexpected time to observe and speculate, she concluded that there was a common link between wrestlers, boxers, marines, football players...and cops. They all looked around and walked flat-footed and braced, as if they believed they could be unexpectedly attacked.

Although the police who passed Penelope were of varying heights and of both sexes, the male half appeared to have been poured into a mold to meet specifications. Their heads were forward, their shoulders and chests were thick and they had strong legs. Obviously a few of the molds had sagged, since there were some potbellies.

Penelope got up and paced restlessly. She was a medical photographer. Lines and angles, light and dark, forms and contrast, fascinated her. She was an artist. She was also plagued with curiosity.

Through the one-way glass panel in his office wall, the detective watched her. He'd glanced at her when she was told to wait there in the hall, and he noted all the details as any good male cop would.

She had rich dark hair down past her shoulders, her makeup was professional, her eyes were green like her long-sleeved blouse, she moved as a woman should, and there were no rings on her left hand. Her skirt was a dark gray, straight, and had a slit up the middle to the backs of her knees, and she wore really stupidly high heels that were the same gray as her skirt. With heels that high, she could break her neck. That wasn't his problem, and he dismissed her.

But he kept glancing up, and that irritated him.

The hall emptied and she looked around impatiently. She stood up, and he got to watch her stretch. Yes. She paced and moved, thinking herself unobserved. She scratched her bottom, and he almost smiled. She looked right at him and narrowed her eyes.

She couldn't know he was watching, but she glanced quickly at the other panels along the hall, then sat down discreetly, carefully crossing her knees and smoothing down her skirt in a very ladylike way.

Now what in hell had made her self-conscious? She hadn't looked at the other panels until she'd suddenly looked at his. Was she psychic? Not that he believed in that, but there'd been a time or two.... Naw. She couldn't have known he was watching her.

He settled back and relaxed, sending benign signals. He was just testing. He wasn't interested. He was doing a study. He mentally poured peace and protection over her. She was in a police station; she had no problems. Then he thought: *why* was she there? A rape victim? He tensed.

She stood up.

Her reaction was so synchronized with his thinking that he was startled and stared. She turned her head quickly, glancing up and down the corridor. Then she looked again at his panel.

His body felt the jolt of her look. Her look heated him, and he wished they were alone someplace with her stripped, caged and isolated.

Her eyes widened and she frowned.

He went back to benign.

But she was restless. She paced. She sat down as two men passed, talking, looking back in quick, interested glances at her as they went on past. She didn't look after the two. That pleased him. Alone again, she stood back up. He felt like Svengali. He sent approval over her, willing his Trilby to sit down.

She didn't. She looked around with intent, darting glances. If he had anything hidden, he would have thought she was going to steal something. Then she held up her hands with her palms away from her, her thumb tips meeting as she "boxed" a view.

As she moved her "view," holding her arms up that way, her breasts jiggled. She wasn't jiggling deliberately. She was alone. That was the trouble with women. They never realized how they interested men just by being there.

He switched the panel off so that it was opaque from his side, too. He got up, straightened his jacket as he walked to his door, opened the door in a positive, businesslike way and walked through. He appeared startled to see her, pausing as if taken aback to see a citizen had invaded the halls of the police station. His surprise was because she was real. He directed his tongue to inquire, "Is someone helping you?" But it came out as, "Are you waiting for me?"

She asked, "About the camera?"

They stared at each other in the empty hall.

She saw that he was one of the mold. With her in her high heels, he was only about four inches taller than she. He was probably thirty—about four years older than she. His thick, rather unruly hair and dark eyes were brown. He looked tough. Unmovable. He had a scar on his chin, and his nose had been broken but not set well.

He said, "Camera."

She recognized that he had no idea about her complaint, so she elaborated, "Mine was stolen. It's expensive, and I have to report it to get the insurance in order to get another one."

"What kind was it?"

"A Leica."

"Yeah."

She knew he had no idea about cameras.

He ventured the comment "You use it in your job?"

"Yes. I'm a medical photographer."

He nodded slightly as he watched her.

She felt guilty. Why should she feel guilty? And she understood it was because she was honest. It was the same as driving down the street and seeing a cop's car. All innocent people feel guilty when they see a cop. She smiled at him.

When he had gathered his wits back into a semblance of order he told her soberly, "I'm Winslow Homer and—"

"You were named for the artist?" She was delighted.

He looked at her. In all his life, she was maybe the third person who had mentioned that. Very few of the people he ran into were familiar with the other Winslow Homer, who was a dead artist. "My dad wanted me to be a baseball player and he thought Win Homer would be good luck. My mom added the 'slow' part and Dad wouldn't speak to her for a year for jinxing me that way. And even now, he says my not being a baseball player was because she put 'slow' in my name." He thought her laugh was delicious. He felt it run through his body like bubbles coaxing something rash from him, like running naked in the rain. It wasn't a clear day, but April was still too cool for nude rain bathing.

"If you are 'slow,' then all the crooks get away?"

"No."

She thought that was true. No one would get away from him, once he set his mind on catching them. "Find my camera. I had some good pictures on the film in it. Actually, it must have been misplaced because I can't imagine anyone taking it. But I can't find it anywhere and neither can Maintenance."

"Where you work?"

"Cottage Hospital. We're enlarging the surgery floor. Of course, I'm not *personally* involved in the enlarging. That was the 'we' of the staff. Actually it's the firm of Lowell and Smithson who are doing all the work." She was babbling.

He just watched her.

"I was being funny."

He nodded soberly.

She checked her watch and sighed impatiently. "I've been here almost an hour. I must have fallen through a clerical crack and been lost. Whom can I see?"

"I'll take care of it. Come in my office." He pushed his door back open and stood aside for her to pass him. He saw that she entered the room briskly and looked instantly at the panel. It was opaque, thanks be.

"Do you get claustrophobic in here?"

"No."

He wouldn't. If he were entrapped, he'd get out, breaking chains or concrete. He could find her camera. "Where will you look?"

He touched the back of her chair as she sat down and he went around the desk to sit in his chair. "Pawnshops."

"Oh. I thought you'd rush right out and pat down all the nurses."

He bobbed his head minutely without changing expression.

She gestured. "What if it's just someone who appreciates the scope of the camera?"

"Camera-scope."

She smiled. He had acknowledged the turn of the word. "Its ability to produce superior pictures?"

He asked again but listened this time. "What kind is it?"

"It's a Leica," she repeated patiently.

"That's German."

He surprised her. "You're a camera devotee?"

"It comes in handy."

"What sort of camera do you use?"

"A Kodak."

"Bird pictures? Flowers?" It was probably for naked women.

"Mostly dead people."

"Oh." She studied him. "Then you're a police photographer?"

"Naw. I'm a detective."

"You take your own pictures?"

"Additional ones."

He would. He'd be thorough. He'd be relentless. He could find her camera. "I particularly want that film back. Please find my camera."

"There are other things we have to do, besides your camera."

That meant he wouldn't find it today. "This week. It would help if you could find it this week. I took the pictures in sequence and I'll have to redo them if the film can't be found. I'm doing a study. The camera has to be somewhere."

"Then you think it's just misplaced, not stolen?"

"I have no doubt it was stolen. I have looked every conceivable place. Even impossible places. It was stolen. 'Borrowed.' Something. I need the camera, but I really need that film. The things I caught were unexpected. I couldn't replace several. Posed, they'd be different. Please find it for me."

"I'll try."

"Good." His "try" would be someone else's promise, she knew that.

"Are you going out to the hospital now?"

She said, "Yes."

"I'll go along."

"Don't you have a car?"

"I'll ride out with you and walk back checking pawnshops."

"Oh." She started to rise.

He drew out a paper and laid it on the top of his desk. "What's your name, address, age, sex, job, Social Security number and marital status?"

She gave him all that, and he was relieved to hear she was single. As long as she wasn't actually married, there was no problem. "Penelope." He tasted the name in his mouth and found he liked it. He realized he'd said her name aloud and explained innovatively, but with the truth, "Names are interesting. My granddad brought my dad up on Babe Ruth. He was a home-run hitter."

"Your dad?"

"Babe Ruth."

"Oh. Baseball must be important to him, if he wanted you to play the game."

"He's a Cubs fan." Homer said that as if it was a complete reply. Then he inquired, "How did you get the name Penelope?"

"My dad named me for a great-aunt of his who was a spinster and had a private income. My mother said, all along, never to wait for someone else's money, to make my own. And I have. Good thing, too. Because the aunt gave the money to something named the Cat House. She thought they took in stray cats."

"I can see how she could have been misled."

"Yes."

He replied soberly, "The lawyer who allowed that, got most of it."

"He died falling down the stairs of the Cat House. His wealthy widow said he was there to see to the dispersal of their windfall."

Penelope swore she glimpsed some dancing lights in Winslow Homer's eyes before he lowered his eyelashes. She'd gotten falling-down guffaws over that story, and it didn't faze this man.

"Your mother's right. Make it yourself."

"I have. I just paid cash for a new car."

He shook his head chidingly. "Don't spread it around that you're solvent. Nowadays men are looking for a woman to support them. The changing times have changed men, and they don't want to carry the workload anymore. They're looking for a woman who'll work her tail off for them, one way or the other."

"Thank you for the warning."

"You're welcome."

His lower lip caught in his teeth and his attention was directed to the paper under his hands, so she saw his eyelashes, which were spectacular and totally wasted on such a man. He glanced up and caught her stare, which he returned. She asked, "Is that all?"

"When did you find out the camera was missing?"

"Two days ago."

"Are the pictures you took candid ones? Were they unposed? Were the subjects aware of their pictures being taken?"

"Mostly."

"Most-ly. Who wasn't aware?"

"A student nurse at a sterilizer. The instruments made good patterns. Uhhh... a doctor before an operation, looking out an open window at the dawn. Beautiful lights and shadows. This camera is so precise that it's like a Brueghel painting. You can take portions of the print and make other pictures. It is remarkable."

He accepted that. "There're others? Those who were unaware?"

"A maintenance man clearing a room. There was a woman helper. I think that was all. The other pictures were of the operations done that day."

"Were any of those people doing anything they weren't supposed to be doing?"

"No. All routine."

"Then we'll try the pawnshops."

"I go along for that?"

"I may need you to identify your property." He made it sound natural.

"They'd pawn it this soon?"

"As soon as possible, before the shops are warned to watch for something. If you're ready, we can go get started. Do you have to check in with anybody?"

"I just handle my assignments."

"Me, too." His face was as usual—unchanging, now concealing his elation. He could be around her for a couple of days and get to know her. Let her get used to him.

He folded the paper with the information about her and put it in his top drawer. After locking the drawer, he rose and said, "Let's go."

With the weather living up to the saying that April showers bring May flowers, the pair put on their raincoats before exiting the police station. At the parking lot he asked, "Which one's yours?"

"The red car."

"Naturally."

With courtesy she unlocked the passenger side for him, and he watched her do that. But he waited to get in the car until she'd gone around the hood, unlocked the driver's door and gotten in. She asked, "Why did you say 'Naturally' when I said mine was the red one?"

"It goes with your coloring."

That put her off-center and she agreed. "How clever of you to guess I did it that way. This red is good with my coloring."

"The perfect way to select a car." He spoke just a tad emphatically, with the tinge of disgust.

So she got snippy and sassed, "Of course."

"What's it get per gallon?"

"I don't know."

"Didn't you ask?"

"They volunteered that information, but I was looking at the upholstery and I forget what they said."

He was sprawled back, wide-kneed and lax, but his safety belt was buckled. He was regarding her with lazy eyes. "You are pulling my leg."

"Yes."

They were silent as she drove with careful skill, showing off, meticulously obeying the rules for driving city streets. He noted that. This Penelope was not the ordinary woman. She would be a handful. Well, he had large hands.

Byford, Indiana, was typical mid-America. For some years, it had been used for opinion polls on various aspects of life. There were marketing agents who used Byford residents to test products, to watch commercials and do surveys. It was interesting. And there were television companies and film studios who used Byford for background shots to give viewers the feel of being in a typical all-American town.

There were spring-budded tree-lined streets, and in yards were brilliant beds of tulips, hyacinths, jonquils and daffodils. The houses in town were modest, made of brick or painted wood, and they were neat and well kept. It was pleasant to drive through Byford.

The hospital had recently been expanded because it was the only one left around that area. Most of the doctors had satellite offices in the little towns fanning out from Byford. The doctors spent a day or two each week in those other offices, but patients had to come into Byford for hospital care.

The expansion of Cottage Hospital's original structure had created a maze of corridors, and going from one section to another could be confusing. That had required hall maps marked You Are Here so that people could find their way.

But Penelope loved it. All the angles and heights made for marvelous camera prints. She was very pleased that it wasn't an efficient octagonal box. She had almost complete possession of that opinion.

So, as she drove her car up to Cottage Hospital with her passenger, she said, "I think this place is just wonderful."

"You would."

"Now, how can you know me that well?" she asked as she deftly wheeled the car into her parking slot.

"I'm psychic."

"Are you, really?" She put the car into Park and switched off the motor as she turned her head to study him.

Homer countered: "Are you?"

"I think I could be, but it scares me a little."

"Why?"

"I like to think I'm in control."

He could agree with that. But he wanted to be the one to control her. He thought he had the beginnings. Look how she'd reacted to him at the station. Perhaps he could lie in his bed and will her to him. Wouldn't that be a feat? Actually, feet weren't what he had in mind, and without changing expression, he smiled over his mental chatter. "Penelope, it'd be best if I'm not introduced as a cop. Okay? Just say I'm a friend who is curious about the changes."

"You want to be covert?"

"Uh." Covert meant undercover. He tilted his head and gave her a quick, all-encompassing glance. "Yeah."

Her own regard was a bit aloof. "All right." She got out of her car and locked her door, then waited as he did the same to the passenger door. When he joined her on the walk, she told him, "I'm called Penelope by my friends."

"I've made the grade?"

She bowed her head slightly in agreement, but she qualified it: "For the covert operation."

"Ah," he said softly. "It's a privilege to be earned?"

"Of course."

"I'll remember that. Don't call me Detective Homer. My friends call me Homer, but my family call me Winslow."

"I'll honor the Friend label."

"I'm honored."

"Don't cut it too thick."

"Don't get your back up, Penna-lope."

"That's a no-no," she warned.

"I guessed that."

"You would."

He repeated her words almost exactly, "Now, how would you know that about me?"

"It figures."

But he wasn't snubbed. He felt they'd successfully passed a barrier in their relationship. That proved he wasn't psychic.

They went into the building through heavy doors that took muscle to move. He handled that for her, but obviously she was used to going through them because she didn't pay any attention. Or probably there was always a handyman around trying to impress her by opening those damned doors to show off his muscles? "Do you have to sign me in?"

"No. I'm cleared, and you're with me."

"I am impressed. Clout."

"I figure if you're a cop and we can't trust you, we're already in trouble. We have to be able to take some things for granted, and I will assume that the police have cleared you. They do tend to want to trust the people they work with down there."

"What if I wasn't a cop?"

"I wouldn't have gone to you about the camera or brought you here."

"Okay, Penna-lope, let's see the scene of the crime."

"I realize this bores you, but the camera and the film are important to me."

"I'm here." He wondered if he'd pushed too much too fast. He didn't know much about women. Just because he was attracted didn't mean that she would be similarly taken with him. He ought to know what he looked like; he saw his face every morning when he shaved. It was only that how he looked had never mattered before. He put his hand up and brushed his crooked nose and briefly felt his scarred chin.

She saw the gesture and looked away. She was too prickly. She was certain that he only meant to tease. She despised to be called Penny or Penna-lope. While this investigation was going on, she could be tolerant and civil. It would only be a couple of days until she could assure the police the camera was stolen and file the insurance claim. She needed her camera.

Cutesy cute Mollie Bronson came along through the lobby and said a sugar-dripping ''Well, hel-lo, Penny. Look what you snagged.'' Then she ignored Penelope and wiggled around and did a toothpaste advertisement with a toothy white smile at Winslow Homer. ''Tell me you're a new doctor and going to do your residence here?''

''I'm a friend of Penelope's.''

He'd pronounced it correctly.

Mollie jiggled and swished around scandalously as if something was wrong with her or bugs were tickling her insides. ''Need an escort?''

''Got one.''

Mollie sniffed. ''She has to read the signs before she knows which way to go.''

With his expression blank, Homer assured the twitching Mollie, ''I chose her because of her ability... to read.''

The pause made it sound as if she had other abilities! What was he doing to her reputation! ''Thanks anyway, Mollie,'' Penelope said. ''You're always so helpful.''

''Any time.'' And Mollie twitched and jiggled away.

''Was she around when they laid out this place?''

''Probably.''

"That could explain the confusion."

"You think she's attractive?" Penelope was indignant.

He agreed. "Distractive."

For some reason, that irritated Penelope. She made a show of knowing her way, but he stopped to read the signs, and she waited silently while he did that. He might be detective-ing. They took the elevator up to her floor and left their coats in her cubbyhole office. There was an adjoining darkroom, which she unlocked and showed to Homer.

He didn't know much about darkrooms. "Do you develop all your own prints?"

"Most. There are some that are tricky, and I have those done professionally."

"This looks professional to me."

He'd given her a compliment. "I took lessons." She had a degree. "Some prints take special fluids that I don't keep on hand."

"But you can develop any prints here?"

"Yes."

"Do you have any that lead up to the roll that's in the camera?"

She moved to a hinged drying rack and showed twelve-by-fifteen prints of various sections of the hospital. Some were of patients, some of ward helpers, some of volunteers. The pictures were superb.

He examined them carefully and took his time. He said, "I hope to God I can convince you to become a police photographer."

That really startled her because he hadn't appeared to be the kind of man who could work with women.

"I like the hospital."

"You'd love crime. It's such a challenge. And the good guys need help."

"Are you a 'good guy'?" She was curious to know how he'd reply.

He answered sternly. "I'm the best of them all."

And she believed him. But that didn't make him palatable. In his work, he was probably honest and fair, but how was he with women? How would he be in the ordinary give-and-take of a relationship? Probably a real pain.

What business was it of hers? Who'd asked her? She'd known him for what, about three hours? And she was deciding he wasn't palatable? He hadn't invited her to taste him. And if he had, she wasn't interested. Not at all. He was a male chauvinist of the worst kind. Well. What did it matter if he was? She wasn't sure. But she *wasn't* interested.

She gave him a cold look and asked, "Seen enough?"

He smiled for the first time and replied, "Not nearly."

She looked at him, disgruntled, watching how his smile changed his blank stern face and warmed his dark eyes. How like a man to become pleasant when a woman has firmly decided to discard him.

Two

Penelope watched Homer in her rejecting way, and saw that he missed nothing. His eyes were busy in a slow, penetrating perusal. *Perusal.* A careful reading. She had never really appreciated the word before then, but that was what Homer was doing. He was carefully reading the room.

What did he see?

Then her own eyes studied the room. As an artist she saw the positives and negatives of space divisions that she'd calculated. She could appreciate her use of the colors, put there for her soul's sake. And she noted that she was somewhat untidy.

While her mind appreciated the jumble of lines caused by carelessly stacked prints, she recognized that her desk and tabletops weren't neat. There were pencils not in their containers. The paper clips were breeding in odd corners like their closet hanger kin.

And she never really looked up as she'd tossed things at the wastebasket. When it came to crumpled papers, "Keep your eye on the ball"—that crucial advice for all sports or business—had never really penetrated Penelope.

She realized that she dressed in the same way she occupied her office. The colors were great, the distribution of interest was careful, her makeup was done with skill, but she did tend to put too many notes or sketches in her pockets, always adding an extra film for her camera. So while she dressed as an artist, she used her clothes as a utility.

Penelope glanced over and caught Homer's perusal of her. He didn't look away. So she couldn't. He was clean and he wore clean clothes. He smelled . . . like a healthy man. Male. Across the room from her, he crowded her. How could that be?

Before then, her breasts had never indicated that they were female. Now she was so conscious of them that she folded her arms to disguise that she possessed anything so pushy. But they pushed right up over her arms as if to call his attention to themselves, and she was embarrassed by their behavior. She couldn't cover them with her folded arms without hunching her shoulders up to her ears, so she turned aside.

He was charmed. In his thirty years, he had witnessed all the tricks a woman could pull to attract a man. And he knew the difference between innocence and calculation. When Penelope had caught him studying her, she had not looked away because she didn't want him to think she was interested. She didn't think she was. But her body was. She'd tried to shield herself from him and could not. She didn't tilt her head and flirt, inviting his interest; she'd turned away, blushing, embarrassed by her body's reaction to him.

He would have to be careful of her. She was going to take some convincing. How did a man go about it? He wasn't at all sure. There had been women in trouble with the law who'd tried to con him into trading sex for help, but he'd never bought that. Not only his morals interfered, but a woman, already in trouble, who'd do that was nothing but trouble for a susceptible male. A man could only lose. Generally when he dealt with a noncriminal woman she was helping, and by that time they were already halfway there.

He wondered if Penelope had ever had a man. His rising jealousy was a surprise. He'd known her now—he looked at his watch—for three hours and twenty-two minutes. How could he be jealous? It was the season. He'd had fresh strawberries for breakfast. In the yards they'd passed, the flowers were blooming. It was spring, and his sap was rising. He'd better watch himself. This one wouldn't stand for a dalliance.

He mused. *Dalliance.* What an entertaining word. To dally. Uh-hum. That would be just great on a day like this, with the wind blowing the trees' new green leaves against the dark blue storm clouds. With the rain beating against the windows, they'd be inside, with a little fire in a fireplace.... "You got any film not developed?" She jerked her head around in surprise. What had *she* been thinking?

"No...not that I recall. I keep all my exposed film in this satchel." She lifted it down from the hook behind the door. "See? This side, the larger one, is new film, and this side is for exposed film."

"It's empty."

"Yes."

"Could film have been taken from that side?"

"I suppose so."

"Could you have put any exposed film with the new film?"

"I doubt it." She went to the drafting table against the wall, gathered the prints and tidied them before she moved them over to lay them on top of those already on her desk. Then she emptied the film onto the table and looked at each roll. All were unused.

He nodded. "It was a thought."

"Do you think, then, that the thief was after the pictures?"

"It's a possibility. We have to think of everything. A camera like that's expensive. It's numbered. It can be traced. Who had it and where. Then who had access to taking it. It would take a stupid person to steal anything so individual, like a camera that different."

"In the time I've had it, there have been a couple of people who have borrowed it over a weekend. It really is a superb instrument. I don't lend the camera to everyone, nor is the offer open to use mine. But there are a couple of people I trust that much."

"Who are they?"

She looked disgusted. "I walked right into that one, didn't I? They wouldn't have to take something they can borrow. None of them would do that without my permission, particularly when the camera's holding a partially exposed roll of film. You don't buy such film for peanuts, you know."

"Any of these people you're protecting work here?"

"Actually, no."

"But the camera disappeared from this place?"

"Yes. I think you're reading more into this than a simple theft."

He was a little ponderous. "We take any citizen's complaint seriously."

"I think your job has made you hyper. You see ghosts."

He agreed, adding: "Of the victims."

She turned then to look at him fully, and her voice was gentle. "We don't always remember that the police have to see the 'bodies' of crimes and how it must affect them. The victims must really haunt you. Especially when the criminal is given every opportunity to escape punishment through technicalities and the victim wasn't given any choice or chance at all. It must gall you when a killer or rapist gets out and kills or rapes again."

"It's never easy." He moved over to the window and looked out over the grounds. With his back to her, he said softly, "So pay attention to this. It's not ordinary. There's something here that makes me restless, and I can't figure out why." He turned and looked at her. "I came along to get to know you. But there might be more to the theft than I thought. This place is secure. Only people who're cleared can come up here. You take pictures of people while they work. You might have taken a picture of something you didn't know was there. Who can get into this room?"

She was still distracted by his saying that he'd come along to get to know her. But she had been listening, so her reaction to his question was only a little delayed as she blinked and replied, "Everybody." She looked around her niche. "This is a safe, serene and friendly place. There are no problems. Everybody here works their hearts out to help other people. They have to feel that way in order to be in this business. No one here is dangerous. I didn't take any clandestine pictures for blackmail. It isn't what you think.''

"Maybe. Any jealousies? Any rivalries?"

"No."

"What about Miss Wiggly downstairs?"

"She's harmless."

Homer grinned. "You did recognize the description."

"She isn't subtle."

"She having any affairs with . . . inappropriate people?"

"She's all promise, from what I've heard, with no putout, I believe is the expression."

"But there's comments about her if you've 'heard.' Who did the telling? Some jealous man? Some hungry married man who'd been teased too much?"

"If you think I have a picture of Mollie copulating with a married man, you're mistaken."

He guessed, "If you'd stumbled onto such a scene, you'd have discreetly backed off and closed the door?"

"I don't open closed doors."

"Afraid of what you'll find in this rampant nest of degradation?"

She gave him a disgusted look and replied primly, "I was taught, as a child, not to open closed doors."

"Your mother and father couldn't leave each other alone?"

"Good grief." She flung out her hands and gave him an impatient look, but then certain memories pried their way into her consciousness, and she smiled a little. She looked down at the table and smiled a little more.

He guessed, "You caught them in the act?"

"No. But you may be right. I stumbled into them in the hall once, locked together and whispering, and Mother laughed in a certain way that—" She straightened and became prim again.

But he laughed in a male version of her mother's remembered laugh. She chilled him with a look as if he couldn't possibly know what she'd been thinking.

"You must come from a *nest* of wild and woolly passion."

"Don't be facetious."

"I take passion serious."

"We're off the subject," she directed.

"Crimes are committed in passion, to conceal something, or for profit. That about covers it all."

"Revenge?"

"That's included in passion. Who do you think could need revenge?"

She flared, "I don't know of anyone in this whole organization who feels the need for any 'crime' at all!"

"But someone stole an expensive camera from you that had a partly used roll of film. Who and why?"

"I don't know!" She was exasperated. "I just need the proof that I reported it stolen so that the insurance company will believe me, pay for it and I can get started again."

He watched the floor as he took a step or two and then looked up at her with his nonexpression. "You want to sweep it under the rug."

"Good gravy, sweep *what* under the rug? Homer, you're making a mountain out of a molehill."

"The insurance company would appreciate a thorough investigation. It's their money."

She put a calming hand on her tilted-back forehead. "Do they call you Pit Bull Homer? You simply do not let go!"

Mildly he agreed, "That's right. Not of anything that I want."

She thought he was looking at her in order to underline the fact that what he had said was about the camera and crime in general.

"Let's go eat. You must be hungry to be so ornery."

She drew in three indignant breaths, and with her lungs much too full, she gasped, "Ornery?"

"I said 'hungry.' Your starving ears misheard."

She expelled the excess oxygen in a very irritated manner, stormed over, snatched his coat off one hook and threw it at him.

He caught it effortlessly, put it over his arm and then calmly helped her into her coat. He even managed to hold on to the abused garment when she viciously thrust her arms into the sleeves. "You don't look at all like a tempered woman."

"If you have any knowledge of human nature, you will be very quiet and allow me to calm myself. You're excessively annoying."

He assured her quietly, "Other people have told me that."

"I'm not at all surprised."

"They were all trying to hide something from me."

She vividly remembered trying to conceal her eager breasts and blushed.

His smooth soft voice asked, "What're you trying to hide?"

Penelope turned to give him a killing look, but he had his eyelids down to slits and all that she saw were those remarkable eyelashes of his, and seeing them tied her tongue. So she just snatched up her purse, got out her car keys and walked ahead of him in long strides. But with her wearing such high heels, he kept up with her without difficulty.

As she drove along, she wondered why she was there. If he wanted to eat, he could have gone down to the hospital cafeteria. She didn't need to accompany him. What was she doing driving away from her workplace with this irritating man and voluntarily going to have lunch with him? She had no idea and wouldn't consider the one that nudged her.

So she was in something of a snit and didn't even ask him where he'd like to go, as any smart woman would have done in that circumstance. She went to Amy's Tea Room. He'd look ridiculous there with all the ruffled curtains and sitting on a chair with a ruffled cushion tied on the seat.

But he didn't look uncomfortable or out of place. Everyone smiled welcomes to him, and he gave his rare smile in return. How obnoxious he was.

He followed her to an indicated table and held the back of her chair as if he was her host. She glanced grudgingly at him and saw he was looking around with his calm evaluation, noting who and what was in that room. Penelope bet that if she blindfolded him and gave him a pen and paper he could write down all the contents of the room. He would be able to do that.

What would he write down about her?

Amy herself came over to the table to be introduced, and she smiled at them both. Waitresses rarely smiled at the female half of a couple. Amy did.

Penelope announced to Homer, "I have an account here. This is on me." Then she glared at him, waiting for his counterclaim.

But the Pit Bull acknowledged the arrangement with a single nod and assured her, "The city treasurer will be grateful."

Amy made a small, nicely amused sound, but Penelope couldn't allow the Pit Bull to know she thought that was funny.

He ordered liver smothered in onions. Penelope ordered the enhanced salad. They sat in silence as he continued his survey. "This isn't at all like you, Penelope Rutherford."

"To buy your lunch?"

"All these ruffles."

"I like Amy."

"Yeah. She'd probably be worth having to put up with the ruffles."

"Ladies like pretty places." She cast down yet another glove of contention.

And he said mildly, "Now, Miss Rutherford, you know you don't like 'pretty.' You like something dramatic."

He was right.

"But I bet you wear frilly lace underwear."

She gave him an outraged stare. He was right again, but he had no business talking to her about her underwear. Her thinned lips pressed together, she pointedly said nothing as she held his stare. Then she deliberately looked aside, to indicate that she was far above such vulgar conversation.

In looking away from him, Penelope saw that he had most of the crowded room's sporadic attention. With his awareness of place and contents, he must know that. She wondered how big his ego must be. And her mind showed Homer like Atlas shouldering the weight of the world, but the Pit Bull's burden was worse because on his shoulders was his colossal ego.

Their meals were brought to their table and placed in front of them. She said, "I don't see how you can eat liver."

He looked at his plate as he should have looked at her, with greedy anticipation. And having verified the who and what of the entire room's population, he could concentrate on his meal. He put his forearms on the table and half-circled the plate as if someone might try to take it away. No one would be so foolish.

She watched as he used his knife to slide slightly browned, translucent onion rings onto his fork, then spear the crisp crust of the fried liver and cut off a bite. She witnessed his mouth opening and saw the pleasure as he tasted the perfectly cooked meat. He chewed as he looked at her, and his eyes smiled into hers. She said to him again, "I don't see how you can eat liver."

He guessed, "You don't like it."

"Not at all."

"Figures."

"I'm a little tired of you saying that when we disagree."

He shrugged. "You're a woman."

"You eat liver." That effectively put him in his place.

He chewed with relish. "Why wouldn't you like something that's this good, that's so good for you?"

"I don't like the smell, or how it looks, or how it cuts, or how it tastes."

"That doesn't leave many pluses."

She almost laughed but managed to remain neutral as she took a bite of her enhanced salad. Then she chewed that as he repeated taking the onions onto his fork, spearing the liver and cutting another bite. As he lifted that to his mouth, she said, "Liver is an organ."

, His fork hesitated.

"It's a mammal's organ. It's not like chicken livers. That's different."

His lips closed around the bite and he chewed. As she prissily took another bite of salad, he asked, "Is your salad okay?"

"Yes. I especially like the crunchy bits."

"Those are grasshoppers."

She lowered her fork and gave him a very enduring look. "That was adolescent."

He rumbled laughter, his eyes spilling with his delight, and she had to blot her lips to hide her smile, but she then had to laugh. He told her, "We may make it, Penelope."

"I do doubt that."

"Hang around and we'll see."

He wanted her to become a police groupie? Wear a leather skirt and put her hair up in strange twists and wear extra rouge? Hardly. He probably meant that she could experience the Case of the Missing Camera with all its exciting ramifications.

"I have read—" she chided the time he was spending on this strayed camera "—that the police have a backlog of cases that is staggering. They're still working on a murder that occurred over twelve years ago. It's no won—"

"Jim Flavis."

"I beg your pardon?"

"The twelve-years-ago murdered man was Jim Flavis. God, how we'd like to find the bastards who did that." He took his plate-protecting left hand off the table and put it, thumb outside, on his thigh as he looked off into an unknown distance.

"Twelve years ago, you weren't a cop."

"No."

"Then how did you get so wrapped up in the case?"

"Cops don't have to know people to try to solve things for them or about them. But I knew of him. He hired one of my friends as a stock boy. That was Pete Gravens who was killed two years ago on a drug bust. Pete was a while getting over Mr. Flavis's murder. I've helped work on that case. All's we have is his murder. No reason. He was a good man. The world's poorer without him."

"I'm sorry."

"For Flavis?"

"For bringing it up."

"Why?"

"You were enjoying your meal, and I've distracted you from that."

He didn't reply but just looked at her. Then he smiled, and it was as if the sun had come out on that rainy day. Her reaction scared her stomach and she became a little big-eyed.

He went back to the liver with evident relish, but she wasn't aware of taking another bite. When she looked down, her salad was depleted. How had that happened?

She rarely had dessert, but he ordered pie. Her plate was cleared form the table, and she sat forward on her chair, her elbow on the table with that hand supporting her chin.

She monitored his careful consumption of the coconut-cream pie, once even licking her lips with a darting tongue when he delayed capturing a stray bit on his own lips. The custard was thick and filled with coconut, and the meringue was piled high, pristine white with the swirls baked to a delicious brown, and the tips of the embedded curls of coconut were toasted. His pleasure fascinated her and when he offered a bite, she took it, and he parted his own lips as he watched her mouth open to enclose his fork. It was the most erotic thing that had ever happened to her in all of her life. It was only belatedly that she understood the pie was just as delicious as he'd made it appear.

As they left and a bemused Penelope was signing the chit, Amy said, "I've sold out on liver and onions. It had to be because of Homer's savoring it with such concentration. But that wasn't all. I was astonished by the dieters who caved in and ordered pie because they saw your expression when you had that bite of Homer's pie." Amy went on to say that she thought the couple ought to come in every other day, and she'd feed them free just to lure people inside to eat too much.

Homer said to count on him. But Penelope was thinking that people had witnessed Homer offering and her taking that intimate bite! Good heavens. By the time that episode had happened, she hadn't even remembered there were other customers. She needed to give closer discipline to her public behavior.

But the wordage in her thinking caught Penelope's attention, and she asked herself just what did she mean by specifying "public" behavior? Did it mean that in private she was going to go berserk? Surely not.

But a wiggle of excitements went slithering around her insides in an attention-getting way.

They went out into the blustery day with its occasional rainsqualls driving them to shelter. He was impressed that she could run on such high heels. She laughed at their scattered dignity and they got a little breathless. That is, she did, and they both got wet as they ran between pawnshops.

Pawnshops were another world. People pawned the strangest things for a few dollars. Penelope picked up a collar bar painted with green moths that no one had ever claimed, but she put it aside as Homer inquired about a hocked camera.

None of the shopkeepers had seen it, that they admitted. Since neither one had expected the camera had been pawned, they weren't surprised not to find it. But Penelope had enjoyed the afternoon. It had been very different. And she liked being with Homer. She liked the way he watched her. She loved it when she could make him smile, when his eyes warmed and he looked at her in that certain way he had.

She took him back to the police station and they said goodbye. She felt a marvelous poignancy because she never expected to see him again. Their lives were so diverse that they wouldn't run into one another anywhere. Like ships in the night they had passed each other. This passing had been on a wild spring day. But their lives would go in opposite ways. She drove back to the hospital in a melancholy mood that fit the day perfectly.

At the station Rick Miller said sourly, "You sneaked her right out from under my nose. I never thought you'd look out of that panel, you're such a recluse in your ivory-tower brain. But you got a peek and moved right in on my territory." His blue eyes were furious.

Homer was shocked. "All I did was help a citizen who was made to wait for over an hour all by her defenseless self in the hall filled with murderers, cops, cutthroats and druggies. All I did was go out and give my protection to a maiden in distress."

Rick said something unprintable through his sneaky black mustache. Then he asked nastily, "Where did you spend the afternoon? Her place or yours?"

"You defame her, buddy. Watch yourself. We went to the hospital to verify the camera was lost, then we went to all the pawnshops."

"I wasn't defaming her. I was hitting at you. Did you find it?"

"No. But you know, Rick, there's a stench to this that makes my ears twitch."

"No bull! What's going on?"

"I don't know. But I have the feeling that it isn't nice."

"With a ... camera? She takes dirty pictures?"

"Hell, man, you saw her and talked to her. You know she wouldn't do anything like that."

"Then what?"

"I hope whatever it is, that it isn't dangerous for her. She's ... something."

"I'd already figured that out by myself. And I'd planned to keep her to myself. Damn it, Homer, why'd you have to horn in?"

"You weren't paying attention to business."

"I was clearing the decks so that I could have the day with her."

Homer nodded over such a plan, and he was very glad that he'd managed to nudge Rick out. "It's the breaks."

"I wish I could break you," Rick snarled.

"It'd take some doing."

Rick glared. "Hell, I know that."

"Behave yourself."

"I'm going to try to get her from you, hear me?"

"No rough stuff," Homer warned.

"Granted."

They shook hands, but Homer smiled like a pit bull.

Three

_____

It was the day after that before Homer called Penelope. The phone rang at six-thirty-one and wakened her. She frowned at the green instrument crouched on her bedside table, then reached over and plucked it from its nest to put it to her ear and ask, "Hello?"

But he didn't say who it was, he just started talking. Only an idiot male with a colossal ego would do something that stupid with a woman he'd just met. He asked, "Have you ever kissed a mustached man?"

"Who is this?"

With the prissy way her voice sounded, they both knew that she knew who was calling. He said blandly, "It's a survey." There were always surveys in Byford. "You curious how it would be?"

"What?"

"Kissing a mustache."

"Who is this?"

She played games. He'd play. "How many men do you take out to lunch in any given week?"

"I haven't kept track."

"You must be hard up to have to spend that much time trolling for some dumb fish."

"Is this Mr. *Herringbone*?"

"Naw. Detective Winslow Homer."

"Detective Win... Oh, yes... you were the one at Amy's with the ruffles—"

"It was the place that was ruffled, not me."

"And you eat fried organs."

He sighed into the mouthpiece so that she could judge the vast scope of his patience. "The city coughed up some legal tender, and I thought I'd repay your hospitality. You free this noon?"

"Let me check." She listened to him breathe into the phone as she lay flat on the bed and looked around the four corners of her bedroom ceiling, there in her parents' house. "If you can make it after one, I can."

"I'll adjust to you."

"What sort of slaughterhouse did you have in mind?"

"How about a seafood place?"

"I can handle that."

"I shall look forward to seeing you, Miss Rutherford." He made the words sound as if he was reading them.

"Shall I meet you there?"

"No. I'll come fetch you at the hospital. Wear a warm coat today. It's gotten cold again."

"Fetch? You imply I'm a stick thrown for a dog."

"Yeah. A pit bull."

He hung up without saying goodbye. That annoyed Penelope. She put the phone back in its cradle, then gave it a pat as she smiled. It was six-forty. What was she doing awake at SIX-FORTY! Ye gods. How dare he call her that early in the morning? She flopped over and wiggled around getting comfortable again.

He had remembered that she'd said he was as tenacious as a pit bull. He was going to take her to lunch. He was going to "fetch" her. Did he really think of her as a stick? She sighed. Her figure was okay. *What would it be like to lie next to him in bed?*

How shocking. What in the world had made her think of that? She'd just met him, and he wasn't at all what she wanted. Not at all. He wasn't.

Then why did the idea of being in bed with him do such interesting things down in the bottom of her stomach? *And why did she want to see what he'd do if she wore that scandalous underwear she'd won playing bridge at Betsy's lingerie shower?*

What on earth had made her think of that outfit? She'd forgotten she had hidden those...where? What had she done with that scrappy, nothing, shocking collection of tangled strings?

She got out of bed to spend some frustrating time trying to locate the outfit. Why was she looking for them?

Well, she was just curious. Times change. In the five years since Betsy almost got married but kept all the shower gifts, the outfit might not be so appalling. Look at the current bathing suits. It wasn't because she was modest that she only wore a racing suit, it was because she didn't want to have to shave the necessary bikini line.

By then it was the normal time to get ready for work. It was a bit late, and she had to hurry, but everyone else was already out of the bathroom and gone. The phone rang and a husky male voice said, "Hello, there." Penelope almost hung up, thinking it was an obscene phone call, but the voice went on, "This is Rick Miller. Remember me?"

What a silly thing to ask. "I—"

"I'm the first cop that helped you about the camera a couple of days ago. When I went to find you, you'd gone. I just wondered if you found it yet."

"No." She rattled her brains to remember a face before Homer's.

"Well, I could come out to the hospital this morning, and we could go over the facts."

"Thank you, but Detective Homer is taking care of that."

"Yeah, I know. He just took over. But, look, I'd like to see you again. Would you have lunch with me today?"

And she remembered that blue-eyed, dark curly-haired Officer Miller had a nice mustache. She smiled. "I . . . couldn't today."

"How about tomorrow?"

"Why, I do believe I'm free tomorrow at noon."

"I'll pick you up at twelve?" he suggested.

"That would be nice."

"Great! See you then. Goodbye."

See? People said "Goodbye" to finish a conversation. If Rick knew that, surely Winslow Homer should. He had no excuse to just hang up when he finished talking.

Penelope showered and dressed in a leaf-green shirtwaist with a wide, dark green belt and green high heels. She did her makeup with particular care and added a little green to the gray of her eye shadow. Not much, but enough to enhance her green eyes.

Just before she left the house, she remembered Homer had said to wear a warmer coat, and she pulled the green plaid woolen one from the closet. She hadn't had to wear it for a couple of days, but the winds were cold again. Trust Indiana weather to be confusing.

By noon Penelope had developed all the film up to the missing roll. It seemed to her that she'd taken more than a partial roll of film. There was too big a gap between subjects. It was as if a whole roll was missing. And she had the smoky almost-memory that perhaps she'd changed the film just before the camera was stolen. But there was no other exposed film roll. Had it been taken, too? She checked her log and couldn't find the book anywhere. My God, she thought. It, too?

If it had been deliberately taken, that would put a whole new face on the theft. To take not only the camera, but the film and log of shots would indicate calculation. What if Homer was right and she'd inadvertently taken a picture of something that someone didn't want preserved on film? What had she seen? But her shot registry was gone.

So just before one, when Homer came up on her floor as if he owned the entire place, she blurted, "My film log is gone. It's the record I keep of who and what and why for each shot."

He stood like a rock and just looked at her. Then he nodded as if he'd expected her to say just that. "Where did you keep it?"

"Here." She went to a bookcase above her drafting table against the wall.

"When did you see it was gone?"

"I had the feeling there was another finished roll of film, and I looked for the log. If I had finished one, I would have put it in the pocket of the satchel. It isn't there. We checked that the other day. And I hadn't logged the shots, so I have no record of them. I'd just finished the roll and hadn't had time for the logging. Do you see?"

"The theft was deliberate."

"Yes."

"What did you see?"

"I've been racking my brains, and there was *nothing* out of the ordinary. I came into the building that morning." She lifted some prints. "See? These were the first of the shots on this roll. Here's the sun almost rising. The few cars. The day's beginning. People already here, preparing for the day, the patients, the operations. This was the basis of all the preparations that are needed. What all it entails to go through the operations."

"Anybody die that day?"

"I don't know."

"Let's go eat. It's past my lunchtime." He let her know he'd inconvenienced himself, delaying his lunch until after one, in order to be with her.

She got her coat off the hook and handed it to him, so he helped her into it. She grated, "I suppose you're going to have kidneys today?"

"I thought I'd try tongue."

"Ugh."

"The greens are pretty with your eyes."

She looked up at him, startled. He'd given her another compliment! She murmured, "Thank you." And then he gave her his smile. It made her a little woozy and the next thing she knew, they were down in the parking lot getting into an anonymous black car. How had they managed to get down there without her having any memory of the transition?

She puzzled over that until they got to the restaurant. There she made a glutton of herself over the platter of all kinds of shrimp fixed every which way, and she was like a cat with its first lick of butter. He could have had lobster brains for all she knew. Did lobsters have brains of sufficient size to supply a meal or would it be like peacock tongues? She shuddered and pushed the problem aside.

That was when Homer decided he'd have her. Any prickly woman who could arouse him just watching her pleasure in eating, had to be a woman of untapped passions. He would waken the sexual storms in her and stir her wild winds of passion. Probably not that day.

With calculation she said innocently, "You asked me this morning if I'd ever kissed a mustache. And I hadn't. But stay tuned. I have a luncheon date tomorrow with a mustache." She carefully dipped one of the last crisp shrimps into some tartar sauce as she waited.

Very satisfyingly, he growled, "Rick Miller."

She raised the pure eyes of a nubile woman and asked in great surprise, "How did you know that?"

"I'm a detective."

"Then," she stated in the satisfaction of knowing she'd provoked him, "we'll find my camera. And that extra film."

"Tell me exactly what you do from start to finish. Begin with loading your camera. Then proceed."

That disappointed her. She had really thought he'd object to her date with Rick. She'd wanted to show Homer that she could interest another man and have

Homer tell her she couldn't keep the date. She'd jumped the gun, trying to make him jealous. They'd only had one day together. He hardly knew her. Why did she think he was smitten just because she was— She was? She was. But he didn't react at all, he just wanted to talk about procedure and processing film. Baloney. How like a man to be so insensitive to a woman.

He read her perfectly. It was interesting to him how the courses he'd had in reading and understanding the criminal mind helped in understanding women. He was going to enjoy the capture and caging of Penelope Rutherford.

He began his campaign. He had her hiding her indignation as he probed her mind for memories of her subject.

She explained, "It's for a book. Some of it will be used as orientation for people having operations. But I plan to publish a full-length book of mostly pictures and the working title is..." She paused for effect. *"The Anatomy of an Operation: An In-Depth Study."*

He groaned almost inaudibly, and she laughed. That was the first ploy. Then he took out a pencil and pad and "found" a small box. He said, "Oh. This is for you," in a very offhand way.

She took the tiny box, expecting gift-wrapped aspirin—he was that kind of jokester—but she found the collar bar pin she'd coveted at the pawnshop. The one of white enamel with hand-painted green moths. She remembered that it had cost a dollar and seventy-five cents. And he had known she would remember how much it cost. It was such a charming, nothing gesture that she was overwhelmed, she was so pleased. She smiled dewily and couldn't think of anything to say, she was that surprised by his gift. She said "Oh" a couple of helpless times and just smiled.

Then he did the third thing. He said, "Please don't go out with Rick tomorrow. You ought not encourage him."

She sat there looking at Homer. He hadn't given her the pin to bribe her into not going with Rick. He'd already had the pin with him when he'd fetched her for lunch.

Homer watched her busy brain assimilating everything and deciding, but he knew he'd won the round when she didn't lose that mushy little smile from getting the pin. He wished it was evening at dinner and he could order a bottle of wine. But it was too soon for this one. She would need time so that she could think she'd made up her own mind.

He had to hold her tiny mirror so that she could pin the bar perfectly on her shirtwaist. She could have gone into the ladies' room to do that, but she preferred to have his attention centered on her as she watched in the mirror and lowered her lashes to look at her chest. Then she asked him, "Is that okay?"

And he smiled in appreciation of her kind of flirting.

She put her hand over the bar and finally said, "How clever of you to know I wanted this. Did you hold up that dear little crook who ran that shop?"

"I threatened him."

She pretended to accept that was so, knowing he didn't work that way. "I love the pin. Thank you."

"You're welcome."

Like a butter-fed cat in the sun, she hardly moved as she stretched discreetly. She couldn't stop her yawn and said in explanation, "I'm so full of shrimp, I need a catnap."

"Let's go to my place."

"Why, Detective Homer!"

"Well, I noticed you didn't have a couch in your office. It must be uncomfortable trying to catch a nap in a spring chair."

"Over the years I have learned to sleep on a high stool with one foot on the floor and an elbow on the drafting table with that hand propping up my chin. I look as if I'm concentrating."

"Ever do it standing up?"

She felt he wasn't talking about napping, but she wasn't going to inquire. She just said "No."

"That takes concentration."

She looked at her demolished plate and blushed a little at her mental image and was willing to agree.

"Especially if you snore."

Oh. He *was* talking about napping. Her mind was going. She'd thought he'd meant—

"Would you like dessert?"

"No, thanks. No room."

"I think you could learn to like liver."

"Don't make me nauseated. Although I hesitate to inquire, what did you have? I don't remember."

"With everything you ate, I couldn't afford anything but the crackers and water."

And she laughed at him.

They went out of the restaurant and she turned up her wide coat collar against the cold wind. Her cheeks were pink and her green eyes sparkled. She liked being with him. He put her into his car and entertained all the impulses of stealing her away and taking her to various other places as he drove back to the hospital.

Penelope hadn't expected him to go in with her. As they went through the corridors, she spoke to the people who spoke to her, but she noticed that they all looked at Homer. It was interesting to see their reactions. The women's were similar. They liked what they saw. The men's reactions varied. They looked interested, hostile, curious and carefully bland, as if they'd been challenged. Men were strange.

She glanced at Homer. He missed nothing.

They went on up to her floor and down the quiet corridor to her offices. As they came to the door, he tugged back on her arm so that he went in the door first. Now, that was sobering. Why would he think she might need protection? He stood looking around, and from behind his shoulder, Penelope looked, too. Then she said "Look," and started to point as someone came walking down the hall toward her door. She half turned to see who was there, and Homer pulled her into his arms and kissed her!

He held her with both strong forearms locked one above the other just above the small of her back, and it was like being held by steel against rock. Her body loved it. Her mouth cooperated and didn't act shocked or surprised at all. The rest of her was both. Her body sizzled with excitements and there were sinuous lickings around that were just amazing. Her head became floppy and her ears buzzed.

There was a male voice that murmured "Sorry." Homer lifted his mouth and looked, then there were footsteps away.

"Who was that?" she asked fuzzily.

"No idea." He smiled down into her wide pupils. "Where'd you learn to kiss that way?"

She stared for just a minute, then the humor crept in and she managed to ask, "How?" So he kissed her again.

But gradually her brain insisted and she moved a little and straightened, not resisting, but needing to speak.

He did seem reluctant to end the embrace, but he lifted his mouth and loosened his arms just a little. Then she knew. "You did that to keep me from saying it."

"Yes."

"The logbook is back," she whispered.

"Yes."

"If you hadn't stopped me from coming into the room first, I probably wouldn't have noticed it was back." Then she asked, "Had you already heard whoever that was coming down the hall?"

"Yes."

"Who was it?"

"I believe it was one of the doctors." Homer described him: "A dark-haired man about medium height, slight, heavy brows and dark beard shadow, a couple of chicken-pox scars along his left forehead, dark-eyed—"

"The anesthesiologist, Dr. Parker."

"Friend?"

"His wife is a lovely woman."

Homer watched her. "Did you take his picture?"

"Not specifically."

"But you took some of the operations on Monday."

She explained: "That was the surgery." Then she told him, "You can let me go."

"I like this."

"But you kissed me to keep me quiet."

"Good idea." And he kissed her again. She wasn't as willing then. Her lips weren't as soft. She was offended to think he'd kissed her only to keep her from telling about the logbook when someone could have heard. His mouth coaxed, but he would have to work awhile to get her back to that impulsive response that had thrilled his body as no woman ever had before her. Her first kiss had been . . . exquisite. He shivered a little, very aroused. "You're driving me crazy."

"Pooh." She released herself from him, separating her body from his.

"There were other ways I could have kept you from saying it."

She smiled falsely. "That was the most effective way." She became businesslike. "Shall I touch it, or will you look for fingerprints?"

"Would anyone, in all this place, have any reason to go over your film log?"

"No. It's only for my information."

"With it back, let's give this place another careful look. Don't touch anything. And if you find the camera, leave it alone. The chances are that whoever took that log has wiped it clean. I would bet even your fingerprints aren't on it."

The camera was cleverly tucked in a corner with her extra boots. It was so casually done that it looked as though she'd put it down there as she'd taken off her coat and boots and just forgotten it. If Homer hadn't gone over the place so carefully just two days ago, Penelope would have believed she had actually overlooked it, and that it hadn't been taken.

"Now, why was it returned?" Homer mused aloud.

"It has film inside."

"How can you know?" He squatted down beside her.

She rose and got a flashlight. "See?"

"Yes."

"I think if I were to develop this roll, I would have duplicates of the pictures in the camera when it was taken. That's why it's been returned. Then there would be no way of proving that the camera had been tampered with in the meantime."

"We have a very interesting problem here," Homer said.

"How are you going to carry the camera and log-book out?"

"I'm not. I'll work on it here." Then he winged it. "I'm loaned to you by your publisher. I'll call a friend I have who is with a publishing house. He'll write a letter dated two weeks ago. He'll fax it to my office, and I'll have it tomorrow. I'm here just to help with the premise."

"I'm impressed."

"I'm not well-known here in Byford, so we'll use my real name. I was introduced to Mollie by it. We'll keep as honest as we can. This may be nothing. A little hanky-panky. But with drugs being what they are, we'll just be sure. And I don't want you alone here. Give it out that you found your camera. Act embarrassed and laugh. Okay?"

"Okay."

"Will you let me kiss you again?"

She tossed back her dark swirl of hair and looked away from him. She even gave a token step or two away. "There's no need."

"Oh, yes, there is."

"We'll see," she said coolly.

"Take off your coat. I'll teach you to look for fingerprints. Then we can develop that film."

She took off her coat and hung it on a hook, then she went a bit further, taking off his gift green moth pin. She reached into her coat pocket for the box, dropped the pin into the little box and slid it back into the pocket of the coat.

He reopened the corridor door to her office and followed her into her darkroom. It was larger than the office. She quite casually removed her dress as if he didn't matter, and put on a smock. She indicated one for him.

"Do I take off my clothes, too?"

"No, just your shirt. Some of the fluids eat materials."

It was some balm to his ego that she slid her eyes over him to check him out. He wasn't ashamed of his body, but he didn't pose for her or tighten his muscles. He put on the smock and it was a little snug. His chest hair showed at the top.

He took up the camera and was careful with such a delicate instrument, but she had the brushes and he carried the powder, so the testing was done. As he'd predicted, not even her fingerprints were on the camera. He would check the log later.

Then she developed the pictures. There were only about four. They were not her pictures, but the angles were exact. Someone had gone to a lot of trouble, trying to duplicate her work. She explained to Homer, "The light is wrong for that time of day. See this angle? It's just a little off-balance. See that shadow? It wouldn't be there. I would have adjusted the angle and the lens. It blocks the hands."

Homer was fascinated, watching, listening. Then he realized she'd shut him out. She was speaking to him as a colleague, not as a potential lover. She was pleasant, brisk, efficient. And she was miles away from him.

Now it would really take time. She just wasn't going to be easy. Damn.

She finished the prints, and she explained that she was going to destroy them because the roll had not been fully used. The only reason they would have developed it, incomplete as it was, would be that they were suspicious of it.

He didn't say he'd already thought of that. He just nodded and agreed. "Can we hide the negatives well enough? If this is a criminal act that someone is trying to gloss over and hide from us, we will need these as evidence."

"They can easily be hidden. I'll take them home."

"Let me. They might look in your house. And Penelope, it kills me, but you're going to have to keep that date with Rick tomorrow. You'll have to tell him you found the camera. We need to quiet any inquiries."

She gave him a stiff side-look and said, "Of course."

The afternoon was gone. She was tired. Still flaunting her indifference, she took off the smock and put her dress back on. She didn't primp but simply ran her hands through her hair to settle it and buttoned up her dress, fastened her belt and put her shoes back on.

He'd taken off the smock and put his shirt back on. He unzipped his pants and tucked in his shirt. He was pleased that the sound of the zipper had made her pause for just an instant.

She handed him the developed film without touching his hand, then she picked up a fresh film, turned off the red light, opened the door and walked into her office. She went over to her coat and dropped the new film into her coat pocket. There was the slightest sound.

He was watching grimly. He saw her hand go down into the pocket, then she hesitated and turned wide eyes toward him as her lips parted in surprise. He went to the door and looked into the hall, then stepped back inside and closed the door. He went to her and hissed, "What is it?"

She withdrew her hand from the coat pocket. She turned it over. On her palm lay two rolls of film.

His frown questioned.

"This one is exposed." She only breathed the words.

"How did it get there?" he whispered.

"It was cold Monday. I wore this coat. I finished the roll at noon, taking pictures from the roof outside the operating room. A different angle. I didn't have the satchel but I always carry extra film." She reached into the pocket along the side seam of the green shirtwaist and pulled out another roll of film. "I put the exposed one into my coat pocket and forgot it."

He said tersely, "Since the camera was taken and returned, and no other pictures are missing, whatever they wanted is on that roll in your hand. Let's get it developed."

"I need food," she protested.

"Okay. We'll go out."

"How about the cafeteria down in the basement here?"

"Okay." He thought that would be quicker. "Then we'll do the pictures."

"I can assure you that there is nothing on this roll that could make anyone nervous. I promise you that."

"Let's be sure." He put the film case in his trouser pocket.

Four

We'll go down the stairs to the cafeteria," Penelope explained. "I need the exercise."

Before they entered the echo-chamber-like stairwell, Homer told her, "We can wait until after we see the prints before we tell anyone here at the hospital who has to know why I'm here. We'll keep it to a visiting colleague if you have to introduce me to anyone."

So he opened the door and a young doctor emerged from the stairs to send a glance past Homer to home in on Penelope. "What are you doing out of the darkroom?" He grinned at her. Then he looked closer at Homer and asked, "Who's this?"

"A loaner from my publisher, Winslow Homer."

"I thought Winslow Homer was an artist. An American watercolorist?"

Homer was manuevering her around the doctor. She exclaimed nicely, "Give the man a purple ribbon." But she laughed a little too much.

"Blue," the doctor corrected. But he smiled, feeling clever.

Homer said staidly, "Blue's for hogs. Purple's for artists."

The doctor had turned, as they had, and taken a step toward them because he wasn't finished with the conversation and Homer was putting Penelope through the stairwell door. "So, you're an artist?"

Before he allowed the door to close, Homer replied, "Yeah. A primitive."

They clattered down one whole flight before the giggles escaped Penelope.

"What?" He gave her a placid look.

Her gaze lifted to his, and the laughter sparkled there. "Primitive." And she laughed again, still going down the stairs.

After another set of steps had escaped upward from under their feet, he said, "Either you think I'm a sophisticated man of élan, or you think I'm a real primitive."

That only set her off again and she no longer tried to smother her delight. The delicious sound rang in the staired tube, and he thought it ought to be taped to fill the emptiness of lonely people. Her laughter wasn't snide; it was just humor. It tickled around inside him, and he grinned at her. That only encouraged her response. There is nothing more infectious.

So he stopped them on the stairs, and he kissed her. He stood solidly—she was in those damned heels— and he held her there and kissed her. And she allowed it. He lifted his mouth and growled, "I just wanted you to know I'm smooth."

"You're going to have to give me an example of your work." He sucked in his breath and his hands had just started to move when she protested, "Artwork!"

He scoffed, took her hand and started back down the stairs. Someone else entered the stairwell above them and came clattering downward, but exited through an upper door. He cocked his head, saying, "There's a lot of traffic on this stair. It could be dangerous. No record of access or egress."

"It's for exercise. Maintenance people are about the only ones who get enough exercise, so they use the elevators. Just about everyone else uses the stairwells. There's a jogging path around the perimeter of the grounds. Maintenance keeps it clear in winter so we can all run. The lazier of us are pushing for a pool."

The cafeteria was a nice buzz of conversation. It was clean and bright. The couple chose from the offerings and found a table. They sat and ate quietly. It had been a long day.

"I'm sorry they didn't have any organs for you."

Without looking up or changing expressions he replied, "I'm going to have yours."

A wave of sensation washed through her, and she could only brace herself in order to survive it. She looked down at her plate and calculated how long it would take them to finish eating and get back upstairs. How could she justify the instant requisition for a couch? She supposed if she specified a king-size bed there would be some suspicions? Wouldn't wiggly Mollie be astonished at pristine Penelope's private ponderings? And she giggled.

Homer's head came around and he said, "What're you thinking? Quick. Tell me." She looked up innocently, and he knew she'd lie.

"I was considering what you could paint as an example of your artistic ability to indicate you're a...primitive. You realize that all you have to do is appear to take it very seriously? You can put a dot on a piece of paper and call it *The Universe in Recession*. Or you can do as one award-winner who painted a canvas black and called it *Before Creation*. It's all in your attitude and the title."

"That's it?"

"That's it."

Along with his food, Homer chewed on the idea. Then he saw that she was finished eating and waiting, and he said, "Okay. Let's go."

They went back up the stairwell. Halfway up, he pretended to sag, and puffed a little elaborately. She scoffed. "If I took my heels off, I could run this."

"Well, I'll just have to see that." He sat down and took off his shoes. So she did, too. "Okay, Pennalope, I'll give you a half-bank start. You'd better *git*."

"I've got to take off my panty hose or they'll be in shreds. Turn your back."

She was wiggling out of them when someone popped in the door. Two nurses hesitated and laughed. "We interrupting?"

Homer said easily, "It's a race. She thinks she's in better shape." And he moved his body just a little.

Penelope was indignant that he would display himself to another woman, and her adrenaline began pumping into her bloodstream.

The two nurses discussed it. "I'll take him," one said.

"Who wouldn't, silly? But Penny is quick. For two flights, I'll back her."

"Fifty cents?"

Homer protested, "Fifty *cents*?"

Someone leaned over the rail on the next landing. "A race?"

One of the nurses replied, "These two."

"I'll take him. A buck."

Homer said to the fifty-cent better, "See? Now there's confidence."

Penelope called out, "On your mark!" And she started up the stairs.

"Hey!" one of the nurses protested. "She's getting away! She's cheating!"

"I allowed her a head start," Winslow explained.

"A hero!" said the other nurse.

"I bet fifty cents on a *gentleman*!" the other protested. She shrieked, and that sound was amplified ringingly in the stairwell.

The stairs rang with the racers, and doors popped open with questionings and the pair were cheered on by the trailing rooters. At the last three steps Homer lifted Penelope and set her down beside him. A tie. All bets off.

Security met them and said patiently, "Racing in the stairwell is forbidden. I'll have to mark you down."

"He's a stranger," Penelope explained. "I was chasing him in order to explain that."

"I see," Security answered gravely. "Just don't let it happen again."

"He understands now."

"Don't I know you?" Security asked Homer.

"I'd remember," Homer replied. "Sorry to've bothered you."

"You make living sound exciting to our patients."
He smiled at the two. "Behave."

Homer gave the man a look and a glinting smile,
making him laugh as he walked away.

Penelope finished putting her heels on her bare feet
and caught the particular sound he had made. "Why
did he laugh . . . that way?"

"I don't know. Want me to run after him and ask?"
He still carried his shoes.

"I thought you were winded. How could you catch
me and even lift me if you were that winded two flights
down?"

"Watching you run excites me."

She could see that reasoning. He was a cop. He
chased people. Wanting to catch people who ran away
was probably genetic. "Are there very many of your
people involved in apprehending reluctant victims?"

He opened the door to her office and gave a quick
look inside as he corrected, "Reluctant victims? No.
Notorious criminals. Beautiful women. Nefarious
creatures. Lawbreakers."

She followed him into the office as she asked, "Why
do you stick women in with all those nasty people,
that— Yeah. Sure. I see. You're a lecher."

"I try." He closed the door after them and said in a
low voice, "Hold still."

She started to smile, but he moved her against the
wall as he looked at the closed door of the darkroom.
He opened that door and stepped immediately inside
as he turned on the light. No one was there.

"What are you doing?" she asked.

"When we left, we left the hall door open. Someone closed it."

She went to her desk and there was a memo on the basket. There would be a spring frolic on the 25th for toys. Buy a ticket, bring a toy suitable for small children. She handed him the memo.

"You assume that explains the door?"

"Yes."

"Okay." He wouldn't argue. "I need a large piece of stiff paper, a wide paintbrush, some red paint and a little black."

"The Picture," she guessed.

"Yes. The Picture. It will be stunning, exciting. It will stir the masses."

"You've known artists." She nodded her head in a series of agreements.

"An oblique writer," he explained.

"They're as peculiar as artists."

"My mother's a knitter. They don't come any weirder than that."

"I have an aunt who's a knitter!"

"Families are riddled with strange people." He said it with satisfaction.

And she laughed.

He almost smiled at her. Then he cautioned, "This creative flame won't last."

She threw up her hands in alarm, kicked off her heels and rushed around, getting the demanded tools for his endeavor. And she loaded her silent, non-fingerprinted camera.

He took off his jacket and rolled up his sleeves as if he were going to scrub for an operation. Then he loosened his tie, unbuttoned his shirt to the waist, and removed his tie. He looked over her crowded hooks and found a scarf. He put that around his neck and flung one end back over his shoulder. Then he mussed up his hair. "I'm ready," he told her gravely.

She was enchanted. She caught it all on film.

She'd set up an easel with some poster board. Alongside was a tray with the poster paint and several sizes of very large brushes. Round brushes. He picked up a brush and stood back. She reminded him, "When you dip the brush in water, you have to flick it at the floor to point the hairs."

"Yes."

But he didn't use water. He used the brush as it was, raw. He lifted the brush, unpointed, botched with red paint, and dashed it against the poster board in an untidy, slanted streak. Then he solemnly added two blurbs at the bottom.

He put down the brush and stepped backward to contemplate the mess. "That's it."

"That's . . . it?"

"Yes." He put his hand to his head as if drained.

She loved it, preserving it on film. There was more to Winslow Homer than she'd ever expected. Then she did a really dirty thing. She prompted, "Tell me about it."

"It's entitled *Astonishment* and it shows the ragged effect of such an emotion on an unsuspecting male. See the frayed edges? See the disorganization? See the hesitation of the climax?"

"Brilliant!"

He took up a small pointed brush of three hairs and dipped it gently into the black. Then he wrote in a spiky script that could look like untidy grass, "Winslow Homer," before he contaminated the brush with the red as he put some tiny, dramatic brushes of black through the disorganized splash of red. The camera noted that.

"Your name source would be proud of you."

"I know," he said with a weary sigh.

"I hadn't realized you had an artist's temperament."

"I try to be ordinary."

And that was when she decided she wasn't going to lunch the next day with Rick Miller.

She took a picture of him lounging modestly beside his masterpiece, his lion's head lifted in patience, his big hand carelessly low on his hip. There were the scarf, the open shirt, the glint in his eyes—all perfectly recorded.

Then she really looked at his work. "Have you had training?"

He replied modestly, "Miss Templeton in prekindergarten."

"She was probably an undiscovered genius." She studied it further. "You know, with that title, there is great meaning to this. You did a spectacular job of it. Did you do it to that word? Or did you name it after you saw it?"

"You have astonished me since I first saw you. I have felt the way that looks: startled, ragged, disorganized, frayed." ·

"Maybe you should quit the cop business and be a writer or an artist. You're good with words, too." She turned from the painting and looked at him soberly. "I'm sure you're from a long line of con artists, and you look so prosaic."

"You insult me."

"That I think you're a con artist?"

He shook his head in denial. "That I look prosaic."

She went to him, laughing, and reached up to tousle his hair more wildly.

With her arms up that way, her body was vulnerable and he pulled her to him, closing his eyes against the thrill of her close to him, and the excitement of her throaty laughter. "You witch."

"Yes," she sassed. "And I have to work my magic...and get that film developed. Give me the roll."

He put his hand into his pants pocket and hesitated. Then he did give her the film roll. He smiled a bit. And his voice was very low and gravelly as he said again, "You witch."

He saw her blink, her smile uncertain. But she hadn't understood her invitation in the way that he thought she was teasing him. She was an innocent. "No woman carelessly asks a man to give her a roll."

She said, "You had it in your pocket."

His smile was rueful.

She frowned a little and then she looked surprised. "'Roll me over, lay me down and...?'"

"Yeah."

She laughed. "Surely I could be more subtle than that."

"Not with me."

"Along with being a con man, I believe you are exceptionally susceptible to women."

"I've never had that trouble before now."

"It's probably a part of the bohemianism that clings to your emerging artistic ability." She considered that.

"Excellent analysis."

She sighed forebearingly. "You're probably going to become a flaming liberal on top of everything else."

"My dad would be shocked."

"Not you?"

"I'd be living it." He made his pronunciation of "living" strong.

She definitely was not going to go with Rick Miller tomorrow for lunch. In fact, she wasn't going to go into that darkroom and spend the evening developing that roll of lost film. She said so.

He judged her stamina and saw that she could do it, but it would stretch her. And he weighed the need to see those pictures. Would twenty-four hours make that much difference? If they stayed longer that night, would someone notice that and wonder at the extended activity in Penelope's darkroom and need to know why? She was probably right. The watcher would know that she hadn't had her camera for those days, he might wonder what she would be doing in there. He said, "Let's go down to the station. We need to see what pictures you took that made someone very nervous."

"Whoever it was is satisfied they are safe. The camera was returned. I'm too tired tonight. Tomorrow will be soon enough to develop that roll of film. You take it with you. I can come by the station and get it in the morning. I'll call you if there's anything that I think will be of interest to your inquisitive mind."

"I'll take you home and come get you in the morning."

"I have my own car."

"I'll follow you home and see to it that everything's okay."

She smiled.

He thought it was in anticipation of him telling her good-night at her place. He smiled back.

She closed down her office, donned her coat and turned up the collar, put on her shoes and stuffed her panty hose into her coat pocket. She carried her camera and the satchel. He watched her like a bird of prey choosing the time to pounce on a mouse. Not a gesture was missed in his regard.

It was dark outside. Cold. "Do you have a fireplace?" His question was a subtle hint.

"Yes." She was trying to match her steps to his stride, and her feet were complaining about wearing heels without stockings, so she was distracted from the subtle hint.

"This would be a great night to sit in front of a fire."

"It would."

He smiled in the dark. There weren't many cars in the lot. He walked with her to her car and saw her get inside. He tapped the window until she first locked her door, then patiently buckled her seat belt. She would have done that anyway. Indiana fined you if you didn't. Then he went over and got into his car.

She drove away, and he followed.

The neighborhood surprised him. He realized single people were buying homes instead of renting. It was logical to accumulate equity in a property and not lose rent money. He followed her into a driveway, and the size of the house was a real surprise.

He pulled in behind her and was unsure. This was more money than a medical photographer could make. He got out of his car slowly and saw that she was already out of hers. He looked around. The grounds were cared for. The neighborhood was a very comfortable one. A dread suspicion crept unbidden into his awareness.

"Can you come in for a glass of wine?" She smiled in a friendly way.

"In front of the fireplace?"

"Of course."

He moved as if he were in hostile territory. They went to the front door, and she used her key. He could hear music inside. It was something classical. "You got roommates? Housemates?"

She looked at him as she opened the door and stepped past, opening it farther so that he felt welcomed. He said hollowly, "You live with your parents."

She smiled. "Yes."

He said grimly, "That figures."

She turned away and called, "I'm home!"

There were vague responses from other places in the house.

"I brought home company!" She allowed Homer to help her with her coat and she remembered to take the panty hose out of the pocket. Then she reached to help him with his coat, but he hesitated. And he was trapped. He hadn't made his move to leave soon enough, and he was going to have to stay the prerequisite twenty minutes that good manners demanded.

Her mother came in, and he saw why Penelope's father had thrown away his freedom and committed himself to marriage. They didn't look alike, but Penelope was just like her mother. And when her father came down the hall, a prickling went up Homer's back because her father was much like Mrs. Homer's bachelor son Winslow.

Down the stairs came a gangly version of Penelope, and Homer felt sorry for a whole decade of males who were younger than he.

They greeted Homer with courtesy, but their love for Penelope was obvious. They really liked her. And she liked them. They were welcoming to him because he was with her. And both parents noted that Penelope carried her panty hose in one hand and they gave Homer sharp looks.

He relinquished his coat, as her parents inquired whether they'd had supper. They all moved into the living room, where there was a fire burning low in the fireplace. Her dad stirred the coals and replenished the wood with natural ease. But then he turned and leaned against the mantel and looked at Homer.

There Homer was, thirty years old, a detective on the local police force, and he felt like a nineteen-year-old with all his sins tattooed on his forehead in pimples. He should have stayed standing.

If he wasn't so gun-shy, their gentle curiosity would have gone unnoticed. But he was a confirmed bachelor and he was a cop. He knew all about questioning. They were excellent and found out all they wanted to know.

They found out he was from Indianapolis. His parents were retired and living in Michigan by a lake. His brothers were all married, scattered across the country. He'd graduated from Indiana University with a degree in criminal justice. He was a cop.

"Detective," Penelope supplied.

"How did you meet?"

That was her father. Yep, he'd want to know that.

Penelope supplied: "I was walking along the intersection at Oak and Pine Creek the other night, and he accosted me."

Her father's patient look rang a bell with Homer. They exchanged the look and each almost smiled. The intersection was a once-notorious hangout for prostitutes.

Since that explanation didn't fly, Penelope amended, "My camera disappeared, and I reported it missing. Homer was nice enough to investigate and found it among my boots in the darkroom."

Homer noted that she didn't want her parents to know there might be a reason for the camera's disappearance. They weren't to worry. She was one of that kind—protective, stupid.

Then, having finished the initial screening, her family vanished with practice that made it seem natural. With them out of earshot, he groused, "You trying to get me shot? Waving those panty hose around that way?"

"Dad isn't hair triggered. He'd inquire first."

"That is a comfort." They were alone in the family protected, insulated living room by the fireplace, and Penna-lope was safe and sound. Damn.

She got him a very good wine and came and sat by him.

"You ought to have your own place. You're too old to still be living at home."

"All the vultures say that."

He was offended.

"I tried the apartment bit. I was lonely, I fought off eager stay-overs, I squandered money on rent, I hated it. So I moved back. I pay about a third of what my apartment cost. I have people over for big parties that

are fun. I have a room of my own. I have support if I
don't want a masher here. I paid cash for my car." She
looked at him. "Two of my friends, living alone, were
raped. One was badly beaten. I don't need that kind
of independence."

He remembered the beating. He'd seen her friend
before they took her to the hospital. Homer looked
around at the pleasant room, the pleasant fire, the
pleasant wine. "I have the feeling we're not alone."

She laughed. Sitting there within hands' reach, she
was relaxed, smiling . . . safe.

"You're what, twenty-six? You're too old to be living with Momma and Papa."

"In whose opinion?"

"You'll be an old maid."

"I don't think so. I have all the natural urges. I'll
find a man who wants marriage. And I'm open to new
experiences. Tomorrow I am having lunch with a
mustache."

She took a sip of wine just as if she hadn't thrown
down another challenging verbal glove. Calm as you
please, she sat there knowing he couldn't throttle her
with her father in the next room, probably with his ear
to the wall and ready to come to her rescue. She was
irritating him. He was never irritated. "If you are curious—" he took a long enduring breath "—I will
grow a mustache."

She looked at him with interest, straightening and
blinking a couple of times to prove that was so, and
she said, "I'm not sure you'd look good in a mustache." That *was* what she said.

He turned with adult patience and put a hand on his
thigh as he eyed her over his shoulder and said, "It's

past your bedtime, Penna-lope. I'll pick you up at seven-thirty tomorrow. Be ready." He rose for his exit.

She said, "In the morning?"

He gave her a shriveling look and replied, "Yes."

Unshriveled, she said, "Okay. I'll see you then. Drive carefully going home. Thank you for an interesting day. I know the pictures are going to be a dead bore, and I really should take my own car. When you have seen the pictures and leave in disgust, I'll be stranded at the hospital and I'll have to take a bus home."

He looked at her and passed on her offer of a release to him. He said slowly through his teeth, "I'll see to it that you get home all right. Safe in the bosom of your family."

"How kind. But if it's inconvenient, I could just ask Rick to bring me home. You needn't bother."

"I may wring your neck."

"That's why I live at home. My dad frowns on anyone else wringing my neck."

"So he is tempted?"

"Now and then, but Mother objects in such a gentle way. Gentle, because he's so much bigger than she." She was being kind in explaining.

"I pity the man you marry. You'll drive him crazy."

"With passion." She said that as if they were discussing the weather. Her brows were raised a little, her eyelids at half-mast, her chin was up and her lips puffed as she nodded in agreement with her own words.

So he kissed her. And she loved it. She melted and wiggled and made tiny, tiny sounds; and he would never again be the same man, no matter what happened to him.

He growled against her lips, "I'm going to take you over behind the sofa and ravish you."

"The dog would find us and bark, thinking we were wrestling over his bone." She shook her head. "It wouldn't work."

"You think I couldn't get you."

"That's why I live at home," she said what was obvious.

"You're a damned tease."

"I am! What do you mean, I am? I was just standing there telling you that you needn't worry about me getting home tomorrow, and you attacked me."

"You're trying my patience," he said through his teeth.

"I haven't noticed that you have any patience at all."

"You are no judge."

"That could be true." She considered such a thing. "I haven't your vast experience with the human race."

"You could be expanded if you were on your own."

She laughed. She laughed the most intimate, soft and secret laugh that he'd ever heard in this life. He sucked in his breath and let the sound soak into his senses, and he shivered with desire. "Tell your parents I wish they were on Mars."

"I shall."

He growled: "I'll see you in the morning. You be ready."

"Yes, sir."

"Good attitude."

"Good night, P.B."

"Peavie?" He frowned.

"Pit Bull."

"Good night, Penna-lope."

And he went out into the cold world and felt oddly bereft.

Five

So the next morning, when Homer drove down her street, Penelope was sitting on the curb, waiting for him. That was exactly where she was. But she wasn't only on the curb; there was a garment bag hanging from a bottom limb of an orderly tree. She was wearing jeans with a sailor's blue pea jacket.

Homer made a U-turn and stopped in front of her, then reached over and opened the door, pushing it so that it swung open. They observed each other. He was disgruntled; she was cheerful.

"The ground's wet and cold. You're stupid to sit there."

She got up, leaned over, straightened and displayed a black pack. "Plastic." Then she reached up and retrieved her garment bag and put it across the back seat. She explained, "My luncheon date with the mustache." Last, she put in her camera, satchel and a small cooler. "Mother made egg rolls."

He watched as she settled herself in the passenger seat, opened the cooler and put a steaming cup of coffee on the console between them. Then she unwrapped the crisp egg rolls stuffed with scrambled eggs, chopped crisp bacon and bits of red and green peppers. Those, too, were hot. His mouth watered. "I'm just coffee in the morning." He waited to be coaxed.

"Good." She began to eat her egg roll as if it were a wiener, holding it in her fingers. Bacon has an insidious aroma.

"I'll try one."

"You get only two. Don't push for a third. Got that? I want my share."

"How many's 'your share'?"

"Three, Just-Coffee-In-The-Morning."

"You're never going to get a husband. You're too nasty and hard to get along with."

"I'm not after you."

That irritated him so much that he ate the two egg rolls without paying any attention to them. But he was belatedly aware they had been well-done, and the coffee was perfect. A sense of well-being came over him. He looked over at her. She was lying back in her seat, one ankle on the other knee, relaxed, female, calmly looking out the window at the passing scene. He told her, "I forgot the roll of film. We'll have to go by my place."

She made no comment. She didn't believe him for a minute. They drove to a very nice complex, and he pulled up in front of one segment in a No Parking zone. How like a cop. He got out and came around to her door. It was locked. She rolled the window down a bit and said, "I'll just wait."

"Come on in."

"Not this time."

"I have a parrot. You'll want to see him."

"Next time." She looked at her watch. "I have to get to work.

He stood there, looking at her, knowing full well that she did not have any schedule at all, and he resisted dragging her kicking and screaming out of the car and up the stairs to his apartment. "I'll be back."

He went up the stairs, unlocked his door and went in and walked to the bedroom and back. Then he went out, closing the door, which locked automatically but which he tried anyway. And he went down the stairs, got into the car and drove away. She wasn't the only one who played games. He'd had the film in his pocket all the while; he was not a man who forgot details. Last night as he lay sleepless, he had planned getting her into his apartment. It had been a ruse, it hadn't worked, and he was annoyed. She just was not easy.

"What's your parrot's name?"

He considered not replying, but he was an adult. "Jacob." He made it short.

"What sort of parrot is he?"

"A macaw."

It was like pulling embedded teeth. "Does he talk?"

"No."

"Good thing."

He looked over at her and there she was, looking so delicious that his innards shivered and nudged. "I cleaned my place last night to show it to you." That wasn't true. He had a cleaning woman, but she had been there the day before.

"Is it any different from any of the other apartments?"

It wasn't. He said in a snide voice, "I don't know. How many other apartments have you been to in that complex?"

"I know several women who live there if you'd like some introductions. None is ready for marriage yet, and they are friendly."

That raised his blood pressure rather impressively. He had never met a dumber woman. She didn't know from nothing. He took some steadying breaths and bit his tongue, so they drove the rest of the way in silence.

"Do you have the letter of introduction?" she inquired.

"Yes."

"But you forgot the film?"

"Yeah."

They walked on into the hospital, up the stairwell and to her office. He stripped off his shirt and put on a smock, and they got to work. She told him what to do and he did that. She developed the film, and they were impatient. As they waited, she suggested that she go ahead and print it out. "That way we can examine the prints more closely without endangering the negatives. All right?"

"Big prints?" he asked.

"How big?"

"Poster size."

"There is no way you could smuggle those out of here. You'd have to examine them here."

He'd already figured that out. "Then that's what we'll do."

"I have a couple of errands. I'll be back in fifteen minutes. If anyone comes along, use the colleague story."

She acted like he was an amateur. "Yeah."

She smiled in a courteous manner, fetched the garment bag from a hook and left. He'd forgotten her date with Rick, and he was in an agony of jealousy. He would go with them. He'd just tag along; that was what he'd do. There wasn't any way, civilly, that they could stop him. He was restless as he waited.

She came back in a flurry and hung up the garment bag. That was when he saw what she had on and he was shocked speechless. He stared. She had on a mid-thigh, spring weight, body-loving knit dress of wide yellow bands separated by narrow dark green lines. It was long-sleeved, a turtleneck, and not long enough. His mouth gaped. If she sat down . . .

"I can print three of the negatives for you before lunch and then—"

"Where's the rest of it?"

She stopped midgesture and blinked as if she didn't know what he was talking about. "The rest of the negatives are in the darkroom." She said that kindly.

Through his teeth he enunciated, "The rest of your *tunic*. Where's the skirt or pants?"

She looked down the form-fitting item in question. "This isn't short. It's midthigh. Twenty years ago, your mother probably wore minis. You're being archaic."

"You're not going out to lunch in that. Rick is a nice young man." He was two years younger than Homer. "You'll spin his head just out of curiosity. That's about as mean as a woman can get. You're to call him and tell him you can't go. Tell him you found the camera."

"I'll handle this my way." She said that like an adult who was in control, and she turned from him and went into the darkroom.

He watched in torn, horrified fascination as she walked away from him in that fanny-hugging skirt with those long legs exposed to other eyes... and she had seams up the backs of those stockings...and high heels. She looked like a tart. A delicious, expensive tart made for one man. And he was going to eat her alive.

He went into the darkroom, closed the door and turned on the red light. He stalked over to her and opened his mouth to continue his tirade—

"I really think these of Dr. Stanton are beautiful. Look at the lines of the window with the slanting shadows of the rising sun. Look at what you can see of his face. It's almost a Picasso Blue Period."

"He looks beat," Homer observed.

"Yes."

"Who were his patients that day?"

"I have it here with the clearances. I can't just take pictures of outsiders, you know. I have to get permission. The first was... It was..." She turned pages. "It was Mrs. Stanton. Cancer. She died on the table."

"Malpractice?"

She looked at Homer. "Why would you say that?"

"Who stole your camera for what reason?

"Yes."

"Did you make duplicates of the negatives?"

"Yes."

"Are they dry?"

"Yes," she replied.

"We'll put them . . ." He looked around the room.
He went out into the other room and taped the thin
strips to the underside of a rubber plant leaf. She was
impressed.

Since the patient had died, Penelope printed the
pictures of the doctor first, enlarging them to poster
size. She did three of the dozen or so negatives on Dr.
Stanton, as she'd promised.

As each print was done, Homer became more conscious of her great talent. The pictures were superb.
Each was a work of art. Her camera talent, the skill of
using such an instrument, plus her eye for line and
contrasts and her artistic ability had created marvelous prints. It was the result expected of everyone who
could aim a camera and snap the shutter.

She never quit in her awareness. She was always as
she had been that first day in the hall at the police station. She saw all the world as subject matter. She
closed an eye to sight, she lifted her hands to frame,
she shifted to see something from a different angle.
And she wasn't doing it for effect. She wasn't acting a
part. It was just the way she was.

So it wasn't immediately that Homer saw the marijuana on the doctor's desk. Only a minute scattering
of several shreds. Then he looked at the cigarette and
saw the gentle shadows of the twisted paper. The
doctor, whose patient had died, was a pothead.

"I can't believe that." Penelope was serious. "Dr.
Stanton would never endanger a patient—a rabbit, a
child, anyone. He would know it would be dangerous
to go into an operating room after having had a toke.
He wouldn't do it. He really wouldn't."

"We'll see who did the cutting," Homer countered.

"I will stake my honor on this."

"Are you his lover?"

"No," she said.

"Why do you side with him?"

She explained, "He would not allow himself to do anything of the sort. I promise that."

"You promised there wouldn't be anything in this roll that anyone would worry about. Malpractice is something to worry about."

"As you said, let's see who held the knife. Oh, Homer, Stanton could *not* do anything like that. I am that sure."

"It would surprise you how many friends and relatives of lawbreakers are that sure," Homer told Penelope. "We'll have to expose this."

"Yes, I know. But before you do, let's see what else is on the roll."

"We can't allow him to operate on anyone else," Homer warned. "The residual of each marijuana cigarette is four weeks. If we conceal this, we are as responsible as he."

"Yes," Penelope agreed to that.

"We need to go to the administrator. He needs to know what's going on."

"I understand. I'll call down and get you a clearance with Dr. Kilroy. He's a good man. He'll be hardnosed about not being informed from the beginning."

"He knew your camera was stolen?"

"Oh, yes," Penelope assured Homer. "I did tell him that, but he doesn't know about the logbook."

"Did you tell him the camera was found?"

"I did as you told me. I said where it was. That you found it there."

"Okay. He has no reason to get huffy. I'll go down now. What time do you meet Rick?"

"At a quarter of twelve in the lobby."

She had lifted her gaze and looked at him. She was telling him the truth. He told her, "You behave yourself. Put your jeans on under that tunic."

"It's a dress."

"It's *almost* a dress."

"You have no sense of fashion." She was impatient.

"I have a strong sense of what's decent."

"I'm completely covered."

"If you sat down . . ."

She went and sat primly, her knees together.

"If you . . ."

She crossed her knees, with skill and discretion.

"If you . . ."

Then she did as Lily Tomlin had done on *Laugh-In*, reprised on *Nick at Night*. Penelope sat prim and trim, but then—as Lily had done—Penelope uncrossed her legs so they were agape, and she stood. Instead of Lily's white utilitarian ones, Penelope wore purple cotton, leg-banded underwear.

He tried not to, but he laughed. He went to her and put one big hand under her chin so that it rested between his thumb and index finger, then he kissed her. His eyelashes were almost hiding his eyes, and his voice was husky as he inquired, "Want to see my parrot?"

"I'll think about it."

Homer went alone to see Dr. Kilroy. He hadn't invited Penelope to go along. She dreaded having Dr. Stanton embroiled in a scandal. But the patient had died. She remembered hearing something about that among the nurses. And there was the echoing comment, "It was a blessing."

Maybe it wasn't carelessness. Maybe it had been meant to be. Penelope looked again at the pictures. Dr. Stanton might look tired, but he looked at peace, lounging there against the window frame, looking out on the dawn. If he really did kill that woman inadvertently, it wasn't wrong in her book. Yes, it was. Oh, how could she judge anyone else?

Carefully, Penelope locked the darkroom. Then she went in search of Mollie.

And down in Dr. Kilroy's office, Homer was hearing that it hadn't been Dr. Stanton who had operated on the morning in question. "He removed himself from the operation. He had a problem and faced it. He'd never smoked pot before an operation, but he knew about the residual effects. He's taking a sabbatical. He'll get help. He's a fine man.

Then Dr. Kilroy said to Homer, "So the camera wasn't misplaced. Security was curious why you were hanging around the darkroom, other than the attractive Miss Rutherford, and Murgurd remembered you from the rape/beating at your apartment complex. You found the guy. Murgurd said you were like a bulldog on that one."

"A pit bull," Homer corrected.

"Yes. I see the difference. Then you knew the woman?"

"No. But I live in that complex. I knew of the people who frequented the place. I realized I'd seen the guy when she described him."

"She is a friend to Miss Rutherford."

Homer nodded. "She told me that just this morning."

"Are there any other of her pictures that could be dangerous to her? I dislike the idea of someone going through her things."

"Me, too."

"Murgurd and the others are watching."

"She'll appreciate that." Homer took a slow step. "We haven't seen the other prints yet. Those will be printed this afternoon. The ones of Dr. Stanton are exceptional in design and balance. It's too bad he's smoking. Instead of appreciating a work of art, he'd only remember the problem."

"He's a dedicated man," Kilroy intoned. "He'll be all right. We'll watch out for him. Other pictures?"

"They look ordinary. We'll have to see them better."

"Keep me better informed."

"Come up and see them."

"Thank you."

"I didn't know if we should trust you," Homer said baldly. "I wasn't sure you weren't involved."

"I understand. The chief tells me that you took this time off. I asked him to count it as investigative, instead of subtracting it from your vacation time. You were obviously devoted to the case."

"Thank you."

The two shook hands solemnly, said goodbye, and Homer went toward the lobby.

Rick was already nervously there. Homer's heart turned black. He stood back in the darkened recess of the side hall, watching. Right on the dot, here came Penelope. Homer straightened. She was wearing the jeans and her smock, and trailing along, peeking around her, was little wiggly Mollie.

Homer watched in astonishment. Penelope shook hands with Rick and gestured, then she turned and indicated Mollie, who stood frozen and *shy* before them. She was dressed in Penelope's scandalous dress. Homer was surprised to see that it looked quite normal on Mollie. Normal! He frowned at Mollie, trying to figure that out.

Then in a lightning bolt of revelation, Homer realized that Penelope *was not going to lunch. She was sending Mollie in her place!*

He moved. He ran to the cafeteria and scooped up an abandoned, half-eaten sandwich and a cup of cold coffee. He made the stairs in record-breaking time that he wouldn't be able to mention. In her office, he ripped off his coat and tie and managed to get to the window to tiredly put his hands into his hair, as she came back.

He turned around and took a startled half-step backward, lifting his hands in surprise. "You didn't go to lunch with Rick?"

She raised her stare from "his" coffee and folded her arms across her smocked chest. "No. Mollie went in my place. I needed to print those other pictures and find another suspect."

"It wasn't Dr. Stanton."

Her sweet lips parted as she asked, "Really?"

Homer nodded. "He removed himself from the operation, and he's taking a sabbatical."

"Oh, Homer, I'm so glad."

"So it wasn't him. It was somebody else."

"Oh."

"Would you like to go have some lunch with me?"

With some droll emphasis, she commented, "I see you've already eaten."

"I could sit with you."

"Do you always drink cigarettes in your coffee?"

He said, "Huh?" And he blushed.

She was charmed. "I saw you in the side hallway, and I wondered why you vanished."

"Mollie looked normal in your dress...your tunic."

Through her teeth she said, "So...did...I."

He shook his head and opened his mouth—

"I shall allow you to buy my lunch."

He nodded, not trusting himself to speak. He put his jacket back on but left his tie hanging on a hook. She tested to be sure the darkroom was still locked, and they went down to the cafeteria.

She watched what he would get but he took a couple of ham-and-cheese sandwiches. She was a little disappointed. She picked up a club sandwich. Then she ordered a malt. He had one, too.

They sat down across from each other, and he looked on her benevolently. "You didn't go with Rick."

"There wasn't time," she replied coolly.

"Don't give me that horse—uh, don't tell me you didn't have time. You're down here with me." He was somewhat arrogant.

"Rick planned to take me to a nice place away from the hospital." She looked prim.

"I would have done that."

"I'm down here with you."

"You didn't tell me you wanted to go out."

"I didn't want to go out," she said contrarily. "If I had, I would have gone with Rick."

He puzzled over that for a while and gave up. "How's your sandwich?"

"Excellent."

His bland expression took full credit.

She added, "The malt's the real McCoy."

"Yeah." He almost smiled.

"I'll probably never know what it's like to kiss a mustache. Mollie took to Rick like a duck to whatever."

"Water. That describes Rick pretty well. Water. He's about that exciting for a strong woman."

"That wasn't a very nice thing to say."

"Why would I be nice about Rick Miller?"

"He's very nice," she declared.

"Yeah. That says it all."

"While you're a pit bull."

He frowned at her. "Only when I need to be one."

"So you admit it."

"I can be somewhat tenacious," he admitted. "When the occasion demands it. But I'm bendable otherwise."

"I hadn't noticed that part," she said primly.

"You never do what you're supposed to."

"Like . . . what?" she asked suspiciously.

"And you live with your folks."

"Fortunately."

"Why do you say that?"

"I don't believe I could fight you off."

"You would want to?" He looked very vulnerable.

"I wouldn't be *able* to."

He frowned. "I don't force women."

"How many have you had?" She was sitting very straight and chewing rapidly, her eyes shooting sparks.

"Very few."

"How many, actually?"

He didn't know how to reply.

"You're taking this long to count them?"

"No. Penelope, for God's sake! Quit being such a damned shrew."

"I?" she inquired in a dangerously soft way.

"Yeah, you." He evaluated her as an honest woman with a conscience. "I'm getting tired of being on the defensive with you. I'm an ordinary man. I'm good at my job. I'm interested in you. Now quit being so damned difficult."

"I'm not the one running around bragging on all the partners I've had."

"How many have you had?" he countered.

"It's none of your business."

"Holy Moses." He looked off in disgust.

There was a silence. Then she said with interest, "I've never known anyone who could do that. You're really very clever."

Baffled, he asked, "What?"

"Snarl silently."

In a narrow-eyed vow, he stated tersely, "I would bet all I own that any man who has ever known you was able to do that. You are more than any ordinary man can handle."

"So," she said with superiority and a good deal of needling, "You can't handle me."

"I said ordinary men."

"Not two minutes ago, you told me that *you* were just an ordinary man."

"I lied." He watched her mutinously. Then he relaxed himself deliberately and went back to eating.

That irritated her most of all, because she was still stirred up. She huffed and moved jerkily.

"You need to get laid."

She reared back and stared down her nose at him. "I beg your pardon."

"That's the first honest thing you've said since I've set eyes on you. But I understand your problem and I forgive you your rotten manners." He waited for her conscience to kick in.

She went back to huffing.

"Just relax. We'll eventually get around to curing you."

She could not think of one quelling thing to say. She was so mad at him that she couldn't sort out her thoughts and get them organized in order to say something that would shrivel him. But there was the niggling little insistent thought that she had been abominable. If their positions had been reversed, she would have walked out on him. Why hadn't he? Of course. He needed to see the prints. That was deflating.

Other than to label her rude and say the cure was laying her, he hadn't ridiculed her or been as nasty as she had been. Why was she acting this way? She had no idea. She felt her eyes prickle and was disgusted with herself.

He said, "I didn't mean to hurt your feelings." Her expression changed so he pushed. "You hurt mine. I meant only to tell that to you. You've ridden over me pretty rough, if you will recall that."

"Where did you grow up?"

"In summers on my oldest brother's place out in Wyoming." Just an unsophisticated country boy.

"Here and there I catch a flavor in your words that isn't Indiana."

"It's close."

"I'm sorry I was rude. You're right, you know, and I have no excuse."

He pushed a little more. "You're needling me like a mare bites a stallion, then kicks up her heels and runs...just a little."

She stared wide-eyed.

"You're attracted to me." He wasn't bragging or swaggering with his words; he was just telling her what was going on.

"I've never behaved like this in all my life with any male."

"That's because you've never wanted any other man," he explained. "Not the way a woman wants a man."

"Then why don't I smile and wiggle like Mollie? I quarrel with you instead."

"You want me to soothe and court you. You almost set me up to fight Rick over you. We had a little black mare out on my brother's place that just about drove us all crazy—us and the two stallions he had. They almost killed each other over her. We had to get rid of her. She liked the excitement. You could drive me wild, too. But I know how to handle you."

"You're going to get rid of me," she blurted.

"See? There you go again."

She put her hands on her forehead and looked shocked. "I really don't mean to."

He countered: "Oh, yes, you do."

"I do not, either!"

"Okay. Okay." He held up his hands."

"Ye gods."

"I'm just glad I got rid of Rick before he was zonked. I'd hate to have to fight him over you, with you standing on the sidelines yelling us both on and enjoying the carnage.''

She corrected: "I got rid of Rick.''

"Yes."

"I wouldn't want you hurt."

He pushed again. "By anybody else. You want to do it personally."

"This is reverse psychology," she accused. "You tell me I'm militant, and then I'll act sweet and simple."

"You found out."

"Yes. Your problem was, you took it just a bit too far."

"You're back in control."

She smiled. "I'm on to you."

"Soon, now."

"If you've finished the lesson for today, we ought to get back to the darkroom."

"Okay. Let's go."

They walked up the stairwell in stately silence. She was very conscious of him, his body, his hands, how he moved, when he looked at her, and she wondered if all mammals were predictable. Could she and her actions be categorized like that black mare out in Wyoming? Pish and tosh. She was a *human* mammal and she was in control of her actions, her emotions; and she knew she could choose her own way.

Feeling independent of the rest of society, above and beyond ordinary behavior, Penelope went into her office and looked back as she said, "I'll unlock the darkroom."

But it was already unlocked: the prints and all the germane film were gone.

Six

How selective of them.'' Penelope was being disgruntled as she saw how cleverly only that particular roll and the few prints from it had been taken. Even the wastebasket had been dumped and checked for any reject prints.

Homer told Penelope, "Don't move from right there. I mean it. Stay right there until I get back. It'll only be a minute. I have to call in."

Penelope leaned against her stomach-high drafting table and frowned. Someone was serious about those pictures. Why? How serious?

Homer came back into the darkroom and closed the door. "Who has access?" He was terse. "Who has keys to this room?"

"Security. Murgurd is head of that, as you know." She gestured to elaborate. "Administration. The fire brigade."

"Anybody else?"

"Who knows? I never before considered boarding it up and womaning the battlements. What's going on?" He was signaling her to be quiet and tapping his ear. He looked around. He mouthed "bugs" and was very serious. He made her impatient.

He said clearly, "All the negatives and prints are gone. We're stymied. Now we'll probably never know what this was about."

"Who are we going to tell that we can trust?" She eyed him solemnly.

"You see the problem."

"What in the world is so important that it's worth all this sneak and snatch?"

He frowned and looked around, again putting his finger to his mouth and ear and pointing to the walls. He sighed hugely and sounded defeated. "We'll probably never find out."

She knew he was talking for phantom listeners. Playing cloak-and-dagger. She felt silly and thought he was being theatrical. Whoever wanted the pictures was someone who worked there, who needed to see there was nothing on the negatives that could embarrass anyone. She didn't take that kind of pictures. Homer was making a mountain out a molehill. She sighed.

He called Security, and Murgurd himself came almost right away. He was interested, unimpressed, and said he'd look around.

Homer called Kilroy, who was astonished. Then he was concerned. "Did you still have the prints of Stanton? I would hate for those to get into the wrong hands."

"The darkroom was locked," Homer reminded Kilroy.

"Yes. But Security here is mostly defensive to strangers. Our people are honest."

"With one or two exceptions," Homer mentioned.

"Uh, yes. What do you plan to do now?"

"I don't know that there's been a crime. The camera was returned. Miss Rutherford states that there was nothing on the roll of film to incriminate anyone, other than the pictures of Dr. Stanton, and he's been removed. So until there is some cause, I'm through here."

Dr. Kilroy agreed. "We appreciate your concern and diligence on this case, Detective Homer. It was a pleasure. I trust this will be our only contact and the hospital will settle down again. Of course, it was never disturbed. Our thanks for that."

"Any time."

"Goodbye, Homer."

"Thank you."

"Well." Homer hung up, his word was resigned. He stretched with stretching sounds and told Penelope, "We might just as well pack it in. You're free, I'm on vacation, let's see the world today."

"Today. The whole world . . . today."

"We'll skip the low points."

She shrugged. Since that couldn't be "bugged"—if there *were* bugs—she said, "Why not? Lead on, Macduff."

Ponderously he confirmed it, "*Macbeth*. Act 3, scene 7, line 12." He blundered through it.

She laughed. "How would I know if that was true?"

He grinned back. "I counted on you not knowing."

As they gathered their things to leave, she asked, "Do you suppose the quoters all realize no one will check on them?"

"No one ever does. Oh, a stickler here and there, but not generally. It doesn't matter enough. The point's been made with the introduction of the idea, so the source isn't that vital."

She put the pea jacket back on, took her satchel and camera, along with her purse, and they went down the stairwell and out to the lobby. There they had to submit to a search.

"We're sorry," Kilroy said in his low voice. "You do understand. We must protect our staff. We need to know that you aren't taking any prints away with you. Copies of the negatives?"

"No," Penelope replied quietly. "All were taken from the locked darkroom."

"You will agree to a search." He smiled at her gently.

"I am surprised by this. If you insist, over my word, I will agree. By a woman."

"Oh, my dear child, of course."

It was a strip search.

As they walked to the parking lot, Homer put his arm over her shoulder quite casually. "Appearances," he said under his breath. Then he added against her ear in a whisper, "Don't discuss this in the car, it could have ears."

The strip search had appalled Penelope. It had also convinced her that someone in that organization had good reason to take extreme precautions to be sure something very wrong wasn't discovered. What?

They drove to the police station and found a secure room to discuss the case with the chief. He was stony faced and frowning, but he listened.

Homer regretfully added, "They X-rayed my clothes so the film's probably dead."

Penelope exclaimed, "You tried to get the negatives out? Where did you have them?"

"In my collar. I should've left them on the plant and let you know where, Bob, but—"

Penelope was big-eyed. "That's special film for airports and so on. It would survive X ray."

The chief narrowed his eyes and commented, "Even strip searches. Interesting. Would they go to that length to protect a pot-smoking doctor's reputation? I would think that would concentrate the scandal, cause more talk as—"

Homer finished it: "As a smoke screen for what's really going on out there?"

And softly the chief added, "What's going on in the town of Byford?"

"How're we going to see if the negatives survived?" He looked at Penelope.

"We'd need special chemicals."

The chief and Homer exchanged disgruntled looks. "And they'd know we got copies out." They looked hopefully at Penelope. "Do you have a darkroom at home?"

"No. I always had free access, twenty-four hours, at the hospital."

The two men's glances met. The chief said it: "We need to get the negatives out of town."

Penelope offered, "I have a friend over in Fort Wayne who has a photography studio. We could use it."

"Good." The chief then told Homer: "You go along as shotgun. We will find Stanton and make sure he's all right. If this should be anything horrendous, we don't know what the ramifications would be. Therefore, take extreme precaution. Switch cars here. I'll have Red do that. You'll have a clean car. It will be... west of here, on the corner of— No, it'll be in Mary Ferris's backyard.

"If you weren't actually followed here, there could be people watching where you went. Your apartments. So you leave here as cops. Wear uniforms. Mary has other clothes. You change there, go to Fort Wayne, and don't call in. I'll ask Steve over in Fort Wayne to act as contact. You can trust him. Okay?"

"Yes."

"The contamination of whatever this is could taint Allen County—if this is what I think it could be."

"Drugs?" asked Homer.

"Yes."

Penelope asked in a still-not-sure-this-is-real tone, "What if it's just hanky-panky."

"To perpetrate a strip search, money and reputations in high places must be at stake. I don't believe any other reason could explain their conduct. If it's simple, we can all sigh in relief. I despise the idea of something nasty going on in this town. Let's be sure. Now tell me exactly where you'll be so that I can provide some sort of protection and backup for you."

They were serious as they changed into uniforms for their departure. They buckled the gun on Penelope's hip, and she looked in the mirror and squinted her eyes in a deadly confrontation.

Watching her, Homer said, "You're scary."

That pleased her. She felt formidable. He pinned the shield on her chest, but he took a while. She gave him a patient look.

The chief told her to put her hair up inside her hat.

She did her hair into a French roll, pinning it securely.

With the hat and dark glasses on, she felt anonymous and lethal—with an empty gun.

"You'll have to leave your purse, camera and satchel here. You can empty what you need from your purse into this police bag."

She cautioned, "There are some precious pictures on the film in the camera." Those of Homer as an artist.

"Do they concern the hospital?"

"No."

"No one will touch them."

When they were ready, the chief told Homer, "Don't worry about anything. We have a contact at the hospital, and we'll keep our finger on the pulse. We'll have people watching any activity out there. Don't do anything but take care of Miss Rutherford. She's your responsibility. Got that?"

"What about my family?" she asked. "If this is as big as you suspect, could someone muscle them to find me?"

"No. We'll take care of everything. We can get some state police to help in a situation like this. We wouldn't use locals who are known at the hospital. Don't worry about anything here. I'll handle this."

She said again, "I still think it's something simple."

The chief said only, "Strip search. That's an invasion of privacy. It's a serious offense."

"I wasn't forced."

"You wanted out of there. You didn't test how far they would go."

"My family...?"

"Don't worry. We'll inform them you're on a special assignment. Fax the prints to us as soon as you can. Go to Steve with the copies. He'll take care of getting the information to me."

They were ready to go. The chief said, "Take it easy. Take care of her. Concentrate on doing just that. If you have to give up the negatives, don't worry about it. We're alerted to something going on out there, and we'll find out what—this way or another."

They shook hands, and Homer left with his disguised partner.

They got an old, dirty car with a perfect motor. They drove it to Mary Ferris's house and into the drive to the backyard. There were other junkers sitting around. "Who is Mary Ferris?" Penelope inquired.

"I'll introduce you."

They got out of the car and went to the back door. They were met by a dirty undershirted, beer-bellied, unshaven, cigar-chewing giant. Homer said courteously, "Penelope Rutherford, this is Mary Ferris."

She extended her hand and said, "How do you do?"

He smiled around the cigar, shook her hand and said, "You staying here?"

Homer said, "No."

Mary replied, "Damn." He cocked his head at Penelope and said, "I suppose you're going to want *clean* clothes."

"Yes."

"I don't know why I always get the picky ones." He led the way to a small, dark bedroom. "Keep the shades down. You got underwear on. Here's slacks and sweaters. A purse. Okay?"

"Thank you."

"You're welcome. Sure you wouldn't like to stay?"

Homer replied from the hall, "No." He came inside the room and said, "I'll help with the equipment."

Mary went out and closed the door. Penelope was a little uncertain. She looked at Homer carefully.

"I'm just going to take the gun holster and belt. The keys and—"

Just outside the window, they heard the back door close and footsteps go down the saggy back steps. Homer said, "Come peek."

She went to the window where the sides of the shade had been curled back by unknown numbers of peekers. She looked out and saw Homer and herself getting into the car they'd come in. She whispered, "Amazing." Then she turned and said, "We could both vanish off the face of the earth and no one would ever find us."

"There are more honest people in this world than you would ever believe. Someone would look for us."

"My family," she agreed.

"And mine," he assured her. "But the police force in this town is one of the best. We're in good hands."

"I can't believe this is happening."

He finished taking off her gun holster and picked up her hat. "Leave the uniform here on a hanger. Leave the shoes on the closet floor. Keep your own things."

She took her heels from the ample police shoulder bag and put them on. She put on the slacks and sweater and felt ordinary for the first time in her life. She left her hair in the French roll. Then she went out to where Homer and Mary stood talking. Homer wore jeans with a jean jacket.

They looked at her in satisfaction, and Homer gave her a kerchief to wear over her hair. And he handed her some dark glasses.

Mary wished them luck and stood silently, waiting for them to leave. He shook hands with Homer and said, "Take care of her."

Homer nodded, put a pair of sunglasses on his own nose, a modified, tired version of a Stetson on his head, and they went out the back door. They walked through the yard and the empty garage, then went out the alley door to the garage across the alley. In it there was a small silver car waiting.

They got in, the garage door opened and they drove out the driveway onto the street and headed west toward Illinois. Penelope objected, "I thought we were going to Fort Wayne."

"We are."

Some miles out of town, Homer took a farm road through a woods, winding around for a long time.

"Do we have enough gas?" Penelope asked.

"Yeah."

After driving a very roundabout way, they finally arrived back east on the south side of Fort Wayne. There they changed cars at a used car lot and left behind Homer's modified ratty Stetson. As they sped away, Penelope saw the silver car leaving the lot, heading south. The man inside wore a modified, ratty Stetson.

Homer then drove around Fort Wayne to the northeast side, then back toward the center of town.

She thought that was all very elaborate, and it would have been tiresome if she'd been with anyone else.

Cynthia's house was in the reclaimed center of town. At Penelope's direction, Homer entered a brick-paved alley. The refurbished carriage house was flush with the edge of the alley. Penelope got out and looked inside. They found one garage stall empty and drove the car into the slot.

They closed the alley doors and exited on the yard side of the garage part of the stable. There was a bricked courtyard with trees of various kinds—big ones at the property line, and small, flowering ones placed artfully in the brick patterns. There were graceful metal, patterned benches also placed with calculation. The original, very large house was at the front of the long narrow lot and was screened from Cynthia's half of the yard by more trees. Cynthia had the courtyard and the carriage house.

It was a place of enchantment. A place to tryst. They ducked under low branches and saw the periwinkles, the lilies of the valley—the small, charming flowers that speak of love. There were pots of scarlet geraniums set to catch the tree-filtered sun. It was damp, there was green moss, and the bricks were old ones that carried the colors of usage, of experience in time.

The red brick of the stable had been tuck-pointed and cleaned. The trim was pristine white, and there was a light burning over the door. It was always lighted. Cynthia said it was Diogenes's lamp. He hadn't needed it after he found her, an honest woman.

She was also a generous one. Penelope knew where the key was hidden, and she put it into the lock.

Homer thought that was a little bold and asked, "What if she has a guest?"

"If it was that kind of guest, she would have him upstairs."

They went into the half of the stable that was Cynthia's studio. Beyond was a kitchen with a small table at one side. Against the alley wall were two easy chairs. In the middle were all the accoutrements needed in an artist's studio, with storage closets at both sides, a freestanding drafting table and a tilted drawing table. It was here Penelope wanted to be. Upstairs was where Homer wanted to take her.

Penelope called up the stairs, "If you're here, so is Penelope and a friend."

But then she found the note.

It was addressed, "To:" And listed were the three people who had her leave to use her house. Penelope's name led. Cynthia said, "Welcome. I've gone to France—April 3—and won't be back for a month— well, May 8—so feel free! Leave me a note. My love to whomever is there. Cyn."

"We can stay here," Penelope told Homer.

He was careful not to rock the boat. He nodded.

She said, "Let's get this printed."

There were smocks. Flamboyant ones, typically Cynthia. And everything was reasonably neat and available. They worked to print out all the negatives, not bothering to enlarge them. All they had to do was get them to Steve and get them faxed to the chief as soon as possible. The prints could be enlarged in Byford for detailed study.

Homer was bathing the prints in the solution. They were making them exactly the right density for faxing. Homer said, "You're very talented."

"Thank you. You can see how mundane these are."

"I think the maintenance couple were interrupted. Look, her dress isn't buttoned."

Penelope was astonished. "How can you tell that?"

"See? It's loose. Her back's to us and it gaps forward." He took another print from the bath and looked at it. "She's missing a shoe in this one, but it's on in that one."

"Aha! The hanky-panky! The chief will be chagrined."

Homer muttered, "There's something about this picture that's wrong."

"Which one?"

"This one you took on the roof. There's something in this that isn't right."

"Not plumb? A hole? A broken window?" She frowned at the print.

"Make enlarged pictures of all these, will you please?"

"Maintenance, too?"

"Yes. All of them," he confirmed.

As the last of the initial batch were drying, Homer called Steve and said the code: "Stand by."

Steve replied, "Ready."

Penelope went through the prints and shuffled them into sequence, then numbered them on the fronts of the pictures.

"You're sure about this sequence?"

"Yes."

"Interesting. I'll be back."

"Do you know how to get back here?" she asked.

"Yes."

"Here's the phone number, just in case. I have to go over to the art school and get some more paper for the enlargements."

"They'll give it to you?"

"I went to school there and I donate to the alumni fund and get the privilege of using the bookstore."

"Good. I worried about discretion in buying the volume needed to replace Cynthia's supplies." He saw Penelope frown and explained, "A large purchase of special paper could be noted. We are the ones who might have copies of negatives, prints of which are interesting to unknown people. As security chief at the hospital, Murgurd could inquire."

"How long will you be with Steve?" she asked.

"I would expect only to have to leave the prints. But if he needs help in the faxing, then I'll do it."

"How will I know? When do I send out the blood-hounds?"

He paused in putting on his jacket. "We passed the strip search. They should be feeling secure."

"Anyone who knows anything about photography knows about duplicate negatives. It's like backup copies for a computer."

"We'll meet here in two hours. That doesn't mean you need to wander the streets until seven o'clock. It just means you're not to worry before then. If I shouldn't come back, wait here. I would have been delayed for some reason. No, no. Nothing frantic. Some prosaic reason. Don't worry about me. I can take care of myself."

"I'll see you at seven, then. I'll have something ready for supper."

"We're staying here?"

"If that is suitable."

He looked around. "This is a dream place."

"Isn't it."

He looked down at her. "Do you have enough money?"

"Yes. For a while."

"You'll be reimbursed."

"No problem."

"Don't cash any checks," he cautioned. "Not yet."

"Oh."

"Is that a complication?"

"No. It's okay."

"Behave. Be careful. Be here when I get back." He kissed her. He held her gently and hugged her sweetly. Then he kissed her again. He repeated, "Be careful."

"You, too."

After he left, Penelope wrote a check for a hundred dollars and opened the secret baseboard, took ten tens from Cynthia's supply and replaced it with the check. Then she went out, locked the door, replaced the key and ran to the bookstore at the art school, barely making it before closing time. The paper was no problem. The student clerk would have been willing to help her carry it home, but Penelope declined.

So she was back to the carriage house in just over twenty minutes. She studied the supplies in the cupboards and the freezer, then thawed a small roast in the microwave. She added a sack of stew vegetables and an onion to the meat and put it into the conventional oven. She went to a grocery on Broadway for fresh supplies, then returned to the carriage house. She took flour, yeast, sugar, salt, eggs, milk and butter and made some dough for rolls, setting it to rise.

With that done, she began to make the enlarged prints of her infamous negatives. As they dried, she looked at the designs of lines and shadows she'd seen in her viewfinder. She found nothing wrong or different or disturbing.

However, she did realize that the maintenance couple, who were married but not to each other, had probably been interrupted annoyingly. There was a packet, his zipper wasn't entirely zipped in one picture nor the belt band buttoned. As the pictures progressed, each had a hand that was doing some self-tidying as they worked: buttons were buttoned, a shoe was restored, hair was smoothed. They were very skilled. They'd been interrupted before. Interesting. They *appeared* normal in their cleaning movements, bed straightening, dusting, but they were restoring their clothing to proper positions all along. If Penelope had not been told by Homer that something had been amiss, would she have seen it? Surely she would have. Someone would have. It would be appalling if she'd printed one in her brochure of how Maintenance functioned!

Now, seeing them as lovers, Penelope looked at them as a man and a woman, and she was curious that they were attracted. But as Penelope studied them, they came clearly across as people who felt and shared. Were they also people who defended their right to behave as they chose? Would they steal negatives and prints? Would they blackmail Dr. Stanton? Penelope had no idea.

When she had come down the hall that day, why hadn't they closed the door? Why had they simply gotten off the bed just as they were? Then they had smoothed it while they had zipped and buttoned what they could as they bluffed it through. Penelope would never have opened a door. The fact that they hadn't

closed it was baffling. Not once in any of the pictures
had the two acknowledged the camera. She had been
so engrossed with lights and shadows that she hadn't
been paying attention to details. Did they think she
would get them fired?

She looked again at the roof print, now enlarged,
that had puzzled Homer. He said something wasn't
right. She looked at the structure, the tidiness, the
clean windows, and she was lost in the myriad lines
and angles with the excellent counterpoint of a truck
parked down at the back entrance. It perfectly cut the
long angle of the edge of the roof. Beautiful. If she'd
calculated that little line interruption, she'd be a genius. She smiled at the composition.

Then she browsed through others. And she found
that the student nurse at the sterilizer didn't have on
rubber gloves. She was removing the instruments with
her bare hands. Didn't anyone do anything by the
book? What *else* wrong were people doing? Here she'd
taken three candid sequences and each subject was
doing something that should not be done. A pot
smoker, a bit of sideline adultery and a stupid student
who didn't know basics! Good grief!

Penelope glanced at the counter and frowned at the
puffed-beyond-all-manner-and-collapsed dough. She
was another dummy. Couldn't even pay attention to
rising dough. She got up, saw it was almost seven.
Winslow wasn't back, and there she was.

She scooped the runaway dough, punched it down,
separated and formed it into rolls and set them to rise
again. They wouldn't be as tender. They'd be good
exercise for the teeth and gums.

She turned down the oven and set the table. Then she went upstairs and looked at Cynthia's bed. It had been stripped and covered with a Holland dustcover.

Penelope smiled and looked around. There was only one bed in the whole living half of the carriage house. It was an enormous room. The bath divided it. There was a sitting room with fireplace at the top of the open stairs. And the bedroom was on beyond, over the garage.

The sofa wasn't the kind for sleeping. Yes, it was. She wouldn't mention that it opened out. She would suggest that since they were both adults they could share the bed. They were beleaguered, and beleaguered people have to cope. He could understand that.

He wasn't the marrying kind. He'd made it obvious. Penelope had avoided his kind. But there was something about an untamable man that was intriguing. She thought maybe she ought to just...taste one. Him. Winslow Homer.

She folded and removed the Holland cover, made up the bed, plumped the pillows and slid a coverlet over it all. It was ready. And she? Was she...ready? She surveyed herself, then went through Cynthia's closet and took out a white wide-legged silk jumpsuit. She put it on and smiled at herself in the mirror.

She heard the car in the alley and went to the window to see Winslow drive up and stop. He got out and looked up at the windows, saw her and lifted a hand to greet her. Then he want to open the garage and put the car away.

She heard the garage door being closed as she ran down the stairs and opened the garden door. He came inside.

"Are you all right?"

"Fine," she replied. "How'd it go?"

"Smooth as glass."

"Then we're home free?"

"Not . . . quite . . . yet. But it's out of our hands. All we can do is wait."

"If they have the pictures, why can't we go back? What could they do now?"

"They don't *know* that we have the pictures. The chief and the state police have to see what's on the prints that's so interesting—why someone went to such lengths to find and get control of them. So we must stay here. Is that going to be difficult for you? I need to watch over you. It's my assignment. You're my responsibility." He wanted to calm any qualms she might have until he could get her into bed.

And she was disappointed. She didn't want him to baby-sit her. She wanted him there to take advantage of an opportunity.

Seven

Penelope indicated the pegs along the wall below the steps rising to the second floor. Homer hung his jean jacket on one of the pegs and set an Ayres shopping sack beneath it. He noted that the floor was uncovered plank boards. It was in very good condition, considering the work done in that room, the chemicals used, the paints and inks.

Then he allowed his eyes to feast themselves on this woman, trapped with him by circumstances he could only have dreamed before this. A dream was possible. She was here. At least for this night. The danger to them was so iffy that it could dissolve into nothing, leaving only a whiff of film-developing chemicals, and she could be back with her parents in the blink of an eye.

This was his one opportunity to live the daydream of any single cop: a delectable endangered female who needed protection. He smiled inside his body. He'd bought enough protection to last a year.

Her sweet lips formed the words: "There's a lavatory under the stairs. Don't carry in a suitcase."

Warned it was small, he went to the narrow door, opened it and shook his head. It was built for a skeleton. Even the door was soundproofed.

When he emerged he said, "I'd like to meet this Cynthia, our blessedly absent hostess."

"Why...blessedly absent?" She gave him a cautious look.

"Where would we sleep another body?"

She didn't know how to reply, so she just looked thoughtful and turned back to needlessly check the baking rolls. They were doing well. They would look like a cookbook illustration. How would they taste? As long as the ingredients were good, there wasn't much one could do to louse up rolls if one didn't burn them. They might not be uniform in shape, but they'd be hot and the butter would melt, and they would taste good no matter what.

And the stew. Good ingredients: add skillet-browned floured meat, tomatoes and onions to a package of frozen stew vegetables, cook at the right temperature, long enough, and presto! It's excellent. No fail.

The meal smelled delicious cooking, and the hot bread was the *coup de grace*. It killed a man's resistance.

She looked over at Homer. He was watching her with a very interesting expression: a possessive one.

He observed, "You've changed your outfit. So Cynthia is your size?"

"Her coloring is different. She's blond and delicate. I find her clothing rather blah. There's a picture of her that I took, upstairs on the alley wall along with some Balinese fans."

He was smart enough not to go up and look at it right then.

"We met at the art school. She's superb. She has flair I could never hope to match, and she knows how to live . . . free. She is gloriously free. I love her."

Cynthia was a free woman, but Penelope lived with her parents.

She opened the wine cupboard and indicated he was to select the wine. He chose, opened a bottle with familiarity and tasted it. Then he handed her the same glass and asked, "What do you think?"

She sipped, moving her eyes as she concentrated. "Perfect. Maybe a little sour. Good."

"You have the palate?"

"No. I watched you."

And he almost smiled as he poured them each a glass. She removed the rolls from the oven and put them into a basket, then she filled the white, curlicue-embossed tureen with stew and set it on the table. She filled the glasses with water, and picked up her wineglass. "Here's to solutions."

"To amiable ones," he amended.

"That's true. One must specify. The solution might be completed and be a disaster."

"What particular problem did you have in mind?"

"Just general. The national debt, the earth's polluted ravagement, the disarmament, who gets the bed."

He laughed a burst of genuine humor. His eyes danced with the lights of it. Since he rarely smiled, even, it was delightful to hear his deep laugh.

"You have a good laugh."

He looked at her for a long minute, then he told her, "You are unique."

"That could mean anything."

He considered that and nodded. But he didn't then go on and tell her why she was different.

He watched her breasts shimmer beneath the soft material and thought he might lose his mind with the wanting. God sure made men easy. Why hadn't He made women as willing? She acted as if they were going to toss a quarter for the bed. "Only one bed?"

"Yep."

"We can share it," he told her. "I have great control."

"Do you?"

She looked startled. Disappointed? All his nerves got excited. "I'll take care of you."

That, too, could mean anything.

He lifted his face and inhaled. "I'm about to die from smelling that good food. When do we eat?"

"I think it's rested enough."

"You made the rolls?"

"Yes. They look a little homemade, but they'll be okay."

"The smell is driving me crazy."

She smiled, very pleased.

"Shall we?" He put his hand on the back of the chair.

"Don't you want to serve?"

"I'll watch." He didn't want the "daddy" role.

She allowed him to seat her then, and she served. She opened a roll, buttered it, then spooned the stew over it, adding extra gravy. He groaned. That helped.

"Where did you get the salad? It's been awhile since Cynthia was here."

"I walked up to a little food store on Broadway. We have strawberries, too."

He decided firmly, "We'll stay here until Cynthia comes back."

"You do know this will be solved by tomorrow. They'll see that the pictures are nothing."

"Did you enlarge them all?"

"Yes."

"That was a lot of work. Thank you. I'm curious to see them."

"You were right about the maintenance couple." She glanced over at him. "I wonder why they didn't just close the door?"

"Then someone might think they were fooling around."

"I'm not sure I would have noticed their...disarray if you hadn't said something about them. Do you think I could have published it and never realized they had been awkwardly interrupted?"

"Any man would have noticed."

"Why...any man?"

"I don't know." He turned out one hand. "It was so obvious to me. I'm surprised you're surprised."

"It bothers me that I didn't know at the time. I wouldn't have taken the pictures. Did you see that they never looked at me? I think that's why they didn't seem...awkward. They were just busy."

Again he laughed. There was such humor in it that she had to smile, too, but her smile was rueful. Em-

barrassed. "I feel naive. Stupid. Unaware. As an artist, I find it especially uncomfortable that I could be
so unseeing."

"You are an innocent," he explained.

"I was so wrapped up in shadows and forms.... It
makes me impatient with myself not to have seen it
immediately. You did."

"I'm a cop. I've been taught to look."

"I'm an artist. I've been trained to see."

"I've been taught to see people. You've been taught
to see colors, patterns, forms, lights and shadows."

"I suppose. But it still makes me feel stupid."

"You're not," he assured her.

"Do you know that the three people whose pictures I took were all doing something they weren't
supposed to, and I didn't even know it? Now, that has
to be borderline stupidity."

"Who else was doing something out of line?" He
held his plate to be served again.

She broke another roll, prepared it and lifted the lid
of the tureen to spoon the steaming stew over the roll.
Then she got up and retrieved the rest of the rolls from
the still-warm oven as she replied, "The student nurse
was taking things from the sterilizer with ungloved
hands. The doctor was smoking pot and the maintenance people were having a little afternoon delight."
She served herself a half roll covered with only a
spoonful of stew. "It makes me want to go back and
look at all the pictures I've taken and see if I missed as
much on any of them. I'm a little disgruntled."

"Still, there is only a personal interest in what those
people were caught doing. The doctor has been solved,
you can give a copy of the picture to the student and
that should shake her up. That leaves only the main-

tenance couple. While they might have reason to get the exposed film and destroy it, they wouldn't have instigated a strip search.''

"That is true," she agreed. "So you're saying there still could be something in those prints that ought not be there? But how could they know? What made them think there might be something on a film that they hadn't seen? The woman who died in surgery would have died anyway. There was no one who could be responsible for the progress of that disease. All the others lived. Not even any setbacks. So why would anyone think there was something I'd taken by accident?''

"We'll look at the prints."

They were silent as they finished the meal. They both cleared the plates away and put them in the small dishwasher. Then Penelope served the strawberries. They had a little more wine and simply relished the treat. As their tongues were satisfied, she asked, "Why are you a cop? A detective?"

"People are interesting. People who go wrong are especially a puzzle. To catch and prevent is a challenge. I don't like people to be victimized. Eventually I'd like to take a wider part in politics. I might run for office.''

"For which office?"

"I'm working on a law degree. I'd like to prosecute the wrongdoers." He gave her a calm look. "I get tired of criminals who get away. Not only the violent ones who do bodily harm, but those sneaks who take things like money or goods or reputations.''

"You've probably lost the criminal vote right there. They outnumber us." He shook his head, but she smiled sourly as she said, "It's time for you to start holding out your hat for contributions. That's the first step. I had twenty letters in three months' time from one candidate who was unopposed.''

"That disillusioned you," he guessed.

"It did make me wonder. Especially since he's been in Congress since before 1980 and can keep leftover campaign funds for personal use.''

"We need to screen our candidates. We need good people. I'm a good man.''

"As with this incident at the hospital, I will be shaken if there is something going on. I've worked there for two years, and I've never seen anything or heard anything whispered that would indicate there is something going on that is wrong.'' She frowned at her last strawberry. "But then I couldn't see anything wrong in the context of the subjects I used that day. You said that I'm an innocent. I think it's more than that. I must choose not to see evil.''

"There are people like that.'' Homer's voice was gentle.

"Rose-colored glasses?''

"Peace. Not having to worry about something you can't control.''

Penelope frowned. "I would dislike being so wimpish that I couldn't protest.''

"I don't think you are. It would take something to get you started, but look how you cooperated with this. You've been a great help. You didn't question leaving Byford and holing up here. You even found us this place. And you've worked your tail off, getting those prints made up. You're a good citizen.''

She shook her head. "There was no decision in doing any of it. I don't believe there's anything really wrong. That must be my blindness. But we keep coming back to the fact of the strip search. I despised that.''

"I was curious what you'd do."

"If I had thought I'd ever be asked to do that...humiliating...exercise, I would have dug in my heels and made them get a warrant or whatever. If I thought about it, I'd become white-hot furious. Why did you submit?''

He shrugged. "It was no big deal for me. And I wanted the copies of the negatives out of there. So it was something of a trade-off.''

"You decided what was important." She looked at him. "What if I'd refused the search? What would you have done?''

"Nothing."

"Oh."

"I know they didn't dare harm you, Penelope. I was listening. One squeak out of you and the negatives wouldn't have made it. But I thought I'd read Kilroy well enough that you wouldn't have any trouble. And they knew I was a cop. Don't forget that. We had some clout. This way, we seemed completely innocent. We got the negatives out.''

"I'm not at all sure it was worth it."

"Let's look. Maybe you can remember something on the edge of your memory that you didn't consciously notice at the time. But Penelope, if you can't think of anything, don't let it weigh on you. You did enough, just taking, developing and printing the pictures. If there's nothing more in them, you've done your share. It is their *reaction* to the possibility that something was done while you were taking those pictures, that has alerted us. We'll watch. If they're up to some mischief, we'll find out what it is. I promise. And Kilroy will get a strip search."

"It ticked you off."

"Yes."

She laughed a delicious, chuffing sound that curled his toes.

When he fought through to reality again, he told her earnestly, "There are good, clever men over in Byford who are going over those prints with a fine-tooth comb. Let's look at these."

They rose from their dessert and cleared the plates away. He started the dishwasher, then he took her hand and put his other hand at the small of her back. "That was delicious. Thank you." And he kissed her.

With her eyes closed and experiencing the sensation that only he had ever caused to riot around in her body, she began to plan other meals, other treats, other bits and trifles that would please him into giving her more kisses.

They took the prints over to the two easy chairs on the other side of the room and sat down. They put the prints in sequence; therefore they began with Dr. Stanton.

"Why didn't I smell it? It has such a distinctive odor. How could I have taken that series of pictures and not smelled the pot?"

"It was cool, so I imagine the heat was on. And it moved in a draft across you and out of the window."

She nodded. "That could be. He looks so tired."

"He'd already decided to give up and get help. So look at the peace."

"But he was having one more." Her tone was cynical.

"He has a real problem." He reached for the next print. "These operations are excellent. I saw a couple of surgical scenes once down in Central America, and I can't tell you how glad I am that I never had to go through one down there."

"Primitive?"

"Difficult situation," he clarified.

"What were you doing down there?"

"I'm in the National Guard."

"Oh."

"We went down there for maneuvers."

"Yes." She remembered reading about that.

"You have no idea how much information you manage to get into one word."

"I learned it from my mother. She is good with glances, too, and she has a stare that is the most powerful force in all creation. She can get a recalcitrant child up out of a chair and off to chores with a look from across the room."

"Terrified you?"

"No. She set off rampant guilt."

"Do you suffer from guilt?" Homer smiled a little.

"Not anymore. I'm an adult."

"But you stew over not seeing that the couple was playing around."

"That isn't guilt." She was impatient. "That's being appalled because I'm that blind. How could I have missed all the signs? Look at these pictures! Every one of them has a clue. God, but I'm stupid."

"Innocent," he corrected.

"I'm tired of being told that."

He gave her his amused, teasing smile.

His smile was riveting. It held her body still while all sorts of marvelous sensations ran around inside her, inside her nipples, licking low inside her torso, sweeping along the backs of her knees, inside her thighs and slipping up the undersides of her arms to peak her breasts. He did that with only a smile. She was susceptible. She was ready.

She looked at him as a potential lover and found she'd looked at him that way since she'd first seen him. Now that was another surprise. And she frowned over the fact that she really wasn't aware enough to see and understand the world around her. She just sort of floated along in her own little groove, not really looking or listening. She must become sharper.

She glanced at him, ready to be whammied by his woman-killing stare.

But he was looking at one of the prints that had puzzled him earlier.

She had taken the shot from the top of the roof adjoining the operating rooms. It was the brilliant one where the long, slanting line of the edge was dissected by—

"This truck. It's something about this truck. What entrance is this?"

She picked up the next print in line, which showed almost the same view, maybe a minute after the first. There was that perfect interruption of the slanted line. Her eyes took pleasure in seeing it again. Marvelous. The truck. Well, it was a big one but not the biggest. It was the kind that ran around town with canvas that was held from flapping with a chain curtain over the back. There was a man standing in the back of it looking down at another man standing beside a dolly on which was loaded some boxes. So? "That's the kitchen entrance."

"What are they unloading?"

"Poison?"

He relaxed and grimaced as if to say "Good gravy."

"How would I know?"

"Look at the truck and the boxes." He was instructing her. "There's something that isn't as it should be. What is wrong?"

She muttered, "How many fish can you find in this picture?"

"Were you any good at those puzzles?"

"It was easy."

"Good. Now, tell me what's wrong with this. I know there's something wrong."

"What could it possibly be?" She studied the print. "They loaded some boxes in a truck, drove it to the hospital, someone pushed out a dolly and they are loading the things from—"

"Penna-lope, you are awesome. That's *it*! See? The dolly handle is on the wrong side. It was pushed out loaded. They aren't delivering anything. They are taking the boxes out of the hospital and putting them into the truck. Let's line up the pictures. Here, put them on the table, side by side. There. See? He's lifting that box up toward the guy on the back of the truck. He's beginning to bend to take it. We have to get to a phone."

"We have a phone." She gestured vaguely in that direction.

"I have to call the chief. I can't have this number on a list. Let's go."

"Where are we going?"

"To a pay phone. What are the numbers on the prints?"

She chuckled. "Twelve through eighteen."

"You were smart to number them. That'll solve communications."

"How?"

Not explaining, he said only, "Let's go."

It was dark, so they took the car. The neighborhood was the sort that no one walked in at night unless he had a big, mean dog.

They found a lighted phone booth and Homer said, "Stay put," and he got out. He wanted her to stay in the locked car, but she got out as he put the change into the phone. That made him a little impatient. So he was distracted from the call and finished punching the numbers quickly and tersely. The phone rang twice.

"Yeah?"

"Stand by." Homer gave the agreed-upon code.

"Ready."

Speaking clearly, Homer relayed the information. "Twelve through eighteen. Dolly handle."

"Ahh. Right. Out."

A car had driven up and stopped across the street. Homer hung up the phone and had taken a tight hold on Penelope's upper arm when two men came sauntering along.

"How about sharing that?" one asked from a distance of about twenty-five feet.

The door of the car across the street opened.

Homer put a bug-eyed Penelope behind him and moved toward their car. She followed and said, "You guys get lost."

"In you," one cheerfully agreed.

She shot back, "Not for a minute."

"Five." They were taunting.

Homer snarled very quietly, "Shut up."

She suddenly realized he was speaking to *her* in that way!

Indignant, she stopped and put her hands on her hips.

A man crossed the street saying, "Break it up. Get lost."

Proving to Homer that she didn't need him, she agreed with the man in the street by adding, "Yeah, Get going!"

Homer took hold of her arm again and began hustling her to their car.

"Who the hell are you?" one of the two accosters asked the newcomer with irritation and some belligerance.

Penelope called back over her shoulder, "You heard what he said. Bug off!"

But the man now at the curb replied gently, "I'm one of the good guys."

"Not like you two," shouted Penelope, who was being shoved into the driver's side of the car and being crowded over by Homer, who snarled, "Be quiet!"

She tried the door on her side, saying, "We can't leave him there. They're after him."

Homer dragged her back, locked her door and snapped, "There's another guy in the car across the street. He doesn't need us."

She looked. And sure enough, the man at the curb was just then indicating the car across the street, and a man got out of the other side of the parked car and straightened very dangerously.

The two accosters made abandoning gestures, raising their hands waist-high in front of them placatingly and walking backward.

The man in the street went back across to the car, and Homer tooted one brief sound, then drove away.

Penelope watched, turning, straining, and saw the rescuer get into the car, and that car went the other way.

"How did you know those two bullies wouldn't jump them? We should have stayed."

In a low and dangerous snarl, Homer told her, "If you ever interfere again when I put you somewhere or tell you not to do something, I will...wring...your...neck. Is that clear?"

Still full of adrenaline, she sat stiffly and said prissily, "I can take care of myself."

He hissed something softly through his teeth. Something about liver. He couldn't possibly be hun— Then she realized he had been asking God to deliver him. She gave him a scathing side-glance and *chose* to be silent.

The silence continued until they were back at the carriage house. She got out and opened the garage doors, but she walked on through to the courtyard, got the key and opened the door, leaving it slightly ajar. She went in and was busily emptying the dishwasher when Detective Homer came inside.

She didn't speak to him. Hell. He was so mad at her, it was probably just as well that she was mad, too. The situation had been in complete control until she'd gotten out of the car. Damned feisty woman.

He could have had one hell of a fight on his hands if those state police hadn't shown up. Their guardian angels. They were real pros. Made it appear as if they were just casual passersby. With the kind of woman Penelope was, he needed extra guardians.

And she hadn't minded him. She'd been ordered to stay in the car and hadn't. He'd had to *tell* her to be quiet ... twice. He'd never had to say that twice since he was sixteen.

She went up the stairs as if she were a queen about to have her head chopped off. Well, he'd make it easy for her. He turned off the lights, checked the windows and doors, and wished for a large, restless dog who'd slept all day.

Out the window, Winslow saw a car drive slowly down the alley, coming toward Cynthia's carriage house. Two men were inside the car. They had powerful flashlights and were looking over the alley buildings. They went on past, and Homer saw the Citizens Watch sticker on the bumper. He relaxed. With them around, the neighborhood was different than he'd thought. It would be safe to go and jog. It might help him. But he couldn't leave her there alone without telling her where he was going. He was tired. It had been a long day.

Upstairs, Penelope was proving the sofa bed really did lift free with one ladylike pull. She had begun to put the sheets on the bed when Homer came up the stairs.

He was shocked to see there was another bed. He gave Cynthia's superb picture on the alley wall a voodoo, ripping glance that she probably felt wherever she was, so he modified it and gave her just a twinge. After all, she wasn't responsible for the conduct of this witch there in that room.

"Another bed!" he exclaimed.

She didn't feel the need to reply.

He tried to help, and she abandoned the job to him.

So . . . he got the sofa bed. He'd never been particularly impressed with this means of lying flat, but it was better than the floor.

She had flounced into the bathroom and closed the door. He sat on one of the overstuffed chairs and contemplated going over, kicking in the door and giving her a slow bath. Deep baths helped women to calm down. Giving her a really thorough one might help him, too. He wished he still smoked. Even that would help. He wouldn't be able to breathe, but he might calm down.

He needed to jog. He'd never get to sleep like this. After quite a while, the shower turned off. Then he was able to speculate what she was drying. Before his mind had finished the job, she opened the door. So she didn't dry herself the way that he would.

Asininely kind, he inquired, "Through?"

Since it was obvious, she made no reply.

He sighed and went to shower and change into some boxer shorts. He'd gone to a mall north of downtown and bought some things. He brushed his teeth, then remembered that he hadn't given Penelope her toothbrush. He went out quietly and walked soundlessly over to her bed.

She was asleep. She sighed. A sound electrified him. A quavering breath. She'd been crying.

Eight

Homer's heart squeezed. He'd made her cry. He was a dog. How could he make up so that she'd let him love her?

Indications had been pretty good. But she hadn't tried to convince him. She hadn't been at the door when he came in just before supper. She might need convincing.

He'd hurt her feelings? Didn't she realize that his patience with her showed he cared about her? If he hadn't cared, he would have just told her politely that she'd jeopardized them both, and if ever there was a next time, to pay attention.

He'd been scared *for* her, not mad *at* her. That was what had made him so rough-tongued. But she'd been crying. She was sensitive to his attitude because she needed a man. Him. She might not realize it yet because she hadn't "seen" it. As selectively observant as she was, she was probably blind to her need for him.

In less than a week? Well, they'd been through quite a bit together. People were tested under stress, just like engines. She was finely made. For the wimp she thought herself, she had been ready to help with an investigation. She trusted him. She hadn't questioned coming away with him. She was ready to help him tackle two rough men who weren't commenting on the weather but on how she'd be used. His ire rose and he shivered with unspent need for action.

He lifted the covers and eased into the wide expanse of Penelope's bed and moved cautiously to the middle of one side. His body became very excited. He had to breathe through his mouth and stay still as she moved to shift position.

There was another shivering sigh from her, and his soul groaned.

Did she dream? Did she feel that he had rejected her? How could she? Then he became aware of his thinking and sighed a long sigh of his own. He'd never thought he'd willingly take on the complication of a woman. They just weren't easy. They were different. So different. Yes.

He'd had his life planned out rather well. Simple discipline would be all that was needed in achieving his goals. He had no need of children. His brothers had provided more than was necessary to continue the contribution of the Homer genes to the pool of humanity. He didn't need a woman in house.

He looked over at the gently sleeping Penelope. She was so...fragile. Even her name held the nuances of ladylike behavior. And she was a lady. Except when she was yelling at the street toughs. He smiled into the darkness beyond her. What a woman.

And he remembered watching her through the one-way panel and her reactions to his watching. Had she really been susceptible to mental suggestion? Why not now?

He looked at her. She was going to be his. How much work would it take to convince her? *Penelope*, he said in his mind, *come over here, now!* And he concentrated, his pupils dilated, his body heated as it tautened with interest. *Penelope*, he thought to her.

She sighed and turned over onto her back, putting her hands up alongside her head.

It worked? *Penelope.* His mind reached to her as he thought her name.

She stretched and turned on her side—toward him!

Was it happenstance? *Come to me,* he commanded with silent intensity and waited rigidly.

She yawned and rolled toward him onto her stomach. He reached out and gently pulled her on over, to her side with her back facing him. Ahh.

Stealthily he enclosed her, moving gently, breathlessly, until he was curled along her back, bringing his knees up under hers, so that they lay spoon fashion. His right hand was spread out over her breasts in a gentle wall. He didn't move.

She turned her head around over her right shoulder and inquired, "Sofa bed not to your liking?"

He froze. She was awake! He mumbled a sound...and quickly decided to act as if he was a sleepwalker and just happened to be there. He said. "Mmm," and kneaded her breasts, running his hand down her body in a feeling swirl, then back up to linger over the pillows of her breasts before going on to her throat. He turned her enough so that he could kiss her mouth.

He did that with consummate skill. And she helped. She wiggled her shoulders, slowly squirming so that she lay flat, with her knees raised and clenched tightly together.

But she hadn't moved away. She was awake and inviting him to make love to her. He couldn't do that as a sleepwalker. He wasn't such a coward. He said, "What are you doing in my bed?"

"It's my bed."

Bending over her, he kissed her deeply, and she accepted it with alacrity. He shivered down his length with longing. His hands explored her, and hers were up behind his head and on his shoulders.

Feeling really sentimental, he said gruffly, "I'm sorry I yelled at you."

"I have the feeling that wasn't the last time you'll do it."

"Then behave."

"I'm not sure I feel that I need always to do as you say. I am twenty-six, and I have made my own decisions for some—"

"Living with Momma and Papa," he said with irony.

"That really sticks in your throat, doesn't it?"

"You ought to be on your own."

That again. "Why?"

"To be self-sufficient."

"I am," she stated.

"Not as long as you're living at home."

"Mother and Dad don't tell me what to do or how to spend my money or anything else. I am my own woman."

"If this was their house, would I be in your bed?"

"This isn't my bed. And no, you would not be in my bed at home. They wouldn't approve. Probably with good cause."

"How many men have you had?"

"Don't be rude."

"I need to know how much risk I run in making love to you," he pushed.

"None." She made it another statement.

"How do you know that?"

"You're my first."

"Yeah. Sure," he scoffed.

"Maybe not."

"Oh, now your memory's kicking in? Now you remember another man?"

"No. You won't be my first, after all." She pushed at him.

"What are you saying to me?"

"Get off!"

"No. What did you mean I wouldn't be your first?"

"That's a simple statement. Anyone with three brain cells ought to be able to decipher it. Get off or I'll clobber you." She was furious. Nose to nose they glared at each other. Through her teeth she started counting, "One...two...three..."

"How many are you giving me?"

"Ten. Four...five..."

"Look, honey, I didn't mean it."

"What didn't you mean?"

"Whatever I said that ticked you off."

She gasped. "You don't remember insulting me?"

If he could keep her talking, she wouldn't be counting. "Penelope." He said her name correctly because now wasn't the time to irritate her. "Honey, you have to know the knots you've tied me in. I need you so bad. Why can't you just relax and let me make love to you?''

"To soothe you," she guessed.

"Yes."

"If I'd soothed every man who needed it, I'd still be busy."

"You didn't do it."

"Of course not. It's a stupid reason to do something like that."

"I love you." That startled him but he smiled down at her. "There's never been a woman who has driven me as crazy as you do."

"Baloney."

"Why, Penelope, how could you be nasty when I just told you I want you?"

"I suppose I'm supposed to be thrilled?"

"Yes."

"Then I'd have to have listened to all the other guys who dusted off that little nugget in order to get me on my back?"

"What a cynic."

"How would you like to be told you were loved by a woman who was only feeling the thickness of your wallet?"

"You had me going there for a minute, but being a cop, the problem's never come up. You don't believe that I could love you?"

"No."

"Kiss me."

"And that's supposed to convince me? All it'll prove is that you've had a lot of experience and you know what you're doing."

"Let me." Then his voice changed, becoming vulnerable and soft. "Oh, honey, let me kiss you," he coaxed sweetly.

She slowly quit the pressure of pushing against him. And she lay quietly, watching him.

He loved her. He held her in a cherishing way, kissing her throat, along her chin, paying court to her ear, her cheek, and finally to her waiting mouth. He did a good job of it. He kissed—softly sipping kisses, then with some pressure—as his tongue caressed for entrance. When she allowed that, he took his time. He tasted, and teased. He gentled and coaxed. He was skilled.

And his hands moved—gently, sweetly, caressing in another way. He slid the straps of her gown from her shoulders, pulling it down to her waist, and lay his hairy chest on her sensitive flesh.

Her toes curled and her heart was not sure exactly which rhythm it was supposed to be practicing. Her skin's reaction was independent of everything else. And she had sensitive places she'd always utilitarianly taken for granted. Such reactions, such hysteria from such odd places! The backs of her knees! How prosaic! The underside of her upper arm? Scandalous! Her inner thighs ached for attention, but he swirled a hand on her hip instead.

"How many woman have you handled this way?"

"Hmm?"

"How...uh...Do that again."

"This?" He kissed her just under her ear, rubbing his evening whiskers there.

"No-o-o, with your hand—"

"There?"

"No. Over a little."

His hand went the opposite way than she wanted. "That way?"

"No!" She was impatient. She reached for his hand, which took some untangling, and moved his hand as she wanted it. "There."

"Like that?" He left it as she'd put it.

"Well, yes. But move it as you did before."

"Like...that?"

"Oh-h-h. Almost."

He loved it. He loved her making him make love to her. She'd forgotten about counting to ten. He moved his hand more insidiously, causing her to moan. He moaned, too.

"Do you have any clothes on?"

He struggled up through fathoms of sensuality and questioned, "Hmm?"

Breathlessly she asked in a scandalized way, "Are you...naked?"

"No."

"Oh."

He offered quickly, "I could be in just a second."

"No. No. I was just curious. I can only feel skin."

He suggested foggily, "Move your hands around a little and see if you can find the cloth." His voice smiled wickedly and he adjusted his body to make the strained cloth available to touch.

But one timid, thistledown hand didn't go down his stomach, it went down his side. That, if nothing else, told him a great deal about Penelope Rutherford. The hesitant touch about ruined Winslow Homer. He sucked in a breath, but his lungs didn't know whether to then exhale or take in more. He became somewhat light-headed, but he was exquisitely conscious of that gentle hand.

As her little hand slipped, inching down toward his waist, he reached quickly, pulled the boxer shorts lower and turned his body more.

Her hand paused. She whispered, "Do you want me to . . . touch you?" She swallowed.

"Oh, yes."

Her hand hesitated, then went lower, then pushed under the waistband. He was so riveted that his stomach flinched and his body jerked with the tension. "Does that tickle?" Her hand paused.

He breathed brokenly and coaxed. "Go ahead."

"It does tickle?"

"No. You excite me."

"Just doing this?" That surprised her.

"Yes."

"Gee, but you're easy."

"Right now."

"You're hairy." She rubbed a slow circle, feeling his texture.

"Yes. But not too much." His voice was strained.

"My word."

His legs moved restlessly but his body didn't, it held very still for her exploration, and he had quit breathing again. "Put your hand around me."

"Oh."

"Ahh."

"It's like velvet stretched over something very hard. Like wood."

He didn't reply.

"What makes it jump like that?"

"It's excited." His voice was a little strained.

"You speak of it as being separate."

"It has a mind of its own."

"How interesting." She put back the covers and sat up.

He allowed that.

"Do you mind?" She looked around her shoulder at him.

"Not at all."

She said, "Oh."

He groaned hollowly.

She said, "How interesting!"

He took air through his teeth; his fingers dug into the bed.

"It's beautifully simple. How amazing."

"You are." He groaned. "Let me make love to you."

"I believe you're . . . ready."

He laughed helplessly, but he could move. He pulled her back down and kissed her with great feeling. His hands moved, and he cherished her.

He seemed to have grown extra hands, and his body was fevered. He touched and smoothed and cupped and stroked until she was almost beside herself. She said, "Don't do that."

"No?"

She changed her mind. "Yes. Do it again."

"That?"

"Oo-o-o."

"Like that?" he asked.

"Yes-s-s."

"Let's just get rid of that."

Her gown was tossed aside. With it gone she felt more of him. His hairy legs were odd against her smooth ones. His stomach was as textured as his chest and it excited her body. She liked it on her.

She said, "Ouch" in a little gasp and froze him midstroke.

"Are you all right?" He panted.

"How odd."

"You okay?"

"I think so."

"Honey, I have to—"

"Push."

"Yes-s-s." And he did. Having sunk himself into the miracle of her sheath, he made an agonized sound of pleasure.

She asked, "Are you all right?"

With her asking a second time in some alarm, he said, "Almost." Then he cautiously moved. When she didn't protest, he moved a little more, and finally he moved to his pleasure, making odd noises, breathing in rasps, and sweating.

Penelope was fascinated. Not *quite* a bystander, more as an involved witness.

She was silent as he collapsed on her, panting, immobile, spent. She waited. He didn't move for some time, and she wondered if he would. He was heavy. When he finally dragged his arms up to brace his weight from her, she moved her head and hands alertly. "Is that all?"

"It sure is."

"Oh."

He put a trembly hand around the side of her head and held it against his sweaty face. "Sorry I couldn't wait for you."

"Well, it was...interesting."

He lifted laboriously, separating from her, abandoning her. Braced on shaky arms he dipped his mouth to kiss hers. "You are the ultimate experience. Thank you, my love."

"Is that an exit speech?"

A little offended, he said gravely, "I've never said that before. I am awed by you." He lay flat in a semi-collapse. "I'm also zapped."

He bubbled a snore soon afterward. She lay frustrated. Then she flopped around several times, but she eventually settled down and slept. She wondered if that was a typical first time. She was disappointed. To have waited this long and been aroused that much, and then be distracted by the mechanics, was frustrating.

With all his grunting and groaning and depletion, she wondered if he felt it was worth it. He'd seemed eager enough. But it had appeared as more endurance and trial than pleasure. Some things weren't in books. Not the ones she'd read.

She was aroused from sleep once and heard the shower. Then she was vaguely conscious of the fact that he was cuddling her bare body against his warmth. It was very nice. She slept and her dreams were erotic. She heated and moved and sighed. And she heard his low, pleased chuckle.

How interesting that this unsmiling man could have such a laugh, and then this naughty chuckle. There were depths to him of which she'd never dreamed. She opened her eyes and turned her head to look at him.

His hands were the hands of a man who works with them. They were hard and callused. On her soft flesh, they were rough textured. The feel of them was exciting to her. He smoothed them down her stomach and rubbed a slow swirl between her hip bones in that protected softness. It gave her pleasure, and she closed her eyes and sounded a long string of mmm's in appreciation.

"Do you like that?" His voice was husky.

She opened lazy eyes and denied it. "Nuh-uh."

He ruffled her hair over her sassiness. "Let me make love to you now, the way I should have the first time."

"I only come into heat every six months."

"Oh." His voice was amused.

"You'd just be wasting your time."

"Not until...October?"

"Yeah."

"I believe it will be very awkward for you, in between times," he mentioned. "You may not be very willing, and I'll probably insist."

"So you think you'll still be around in October?"

"I'll have to see."

"This is a test," she guessed.

"Yep."

"You want me to fake it?"

"That might be best," he confided kindly. "Do you think you can?"

"I'll have to see."

He leaned his head down, and his hand gently squeezed her breast as his opened mouth reached her nipple. She watched that and gasped over the sensation. He suckled, pulling hard. Her body reacted, moving languorously, sinuously.

His hand moved down her stomach into her crisp curls and a finger slid farther. He lifted his head and said softly, "It's October."

"Where does the time go?"

He tumbled her around as he rolled her and tasted her and played with her. And he made love to her. He did it beautifully, and she squirmed and wiggled and helped.

He teased her to passion, thrilling her into shivers, then he led her up that spiral of ecstasy to climax. She clung to him, and he held her tightly so that she didn't actually fly into a million pieces, but she had thought that she might.

When she could speak coherently, she gasped, "So that's what it's all about."

"Almost."

"There's more?" She clutched at the sheet.

He looked off to the side as he explained, "You have to propose to me."

"I was just playing," she protested.

"But I took your advances seriously, and I have my reputation to protect. You can't just fool around and go your way."

"Trapped?"

He promised: "It's that or my daddy gets out the shotgun."

She laughed delightedly. Then she told him, "You're so funny. I never expected your humor. Actually, Detective Homer, I really didn't think women particularly interested you."

He looked at her blankly. "I surprised you?"

"Well, not in your interest in sex, but your teasing about getting married is rash. What if I took you seriously?"

"How do you know I'm not?"

She shook her head. "You're not the marrying kind."

"What kind is that?"

"A woman can tell. Men act differently when they are serious."

"They stay on the sofa bed?"

She laughed again. "There you go again. You're really humorous."

"We haven't known each other very long. Will you go with me? You need to meet my parrot."

"Where did you get a parrot?"

"It was a gift."

"And it doesn't talk?"

"Not a word," he promised.

"I thought the purpose of having a parrot was to teach it to say, 'Birds can't talk.' They have a mynah bird, here, at the Children's Zoo in Fort Wayne that says that. I think it was brilliant to teach a bird to say that particular phrase. What a sense of humor."

He agreed. "Whoever did teach the bird must love standing there and watching it talk to people."

"Yes. I wonder if he or she does."

"You would." He knew that would be so.

"I wouldn't be so clever as to think of such a good joke. You have marvelous humor. You seem so positive. So...staid and in control. I really have seen a different man in these last twenty-four hours. You're really rather rash."

"I'm not ordinarily. You rouse a different man."

She said, "I need to be kissed."

"I have one left," he admitted in a defeated way.

"A good thing."

He had more than one.

By then it was almost dawn, and the phone rang. The lovers exchanged a look, then Homer reached and answered it. He said, "Ready."

And Steve replied, "Stand by. I'm coming over."

Homer hung up softly, frowning. "It must be important. Let's get dressed."

They flung back the covers and took turns in the bathroom, and he gave her the new toothbrush he'd bought for her. They dressed in the clothes they'd worn there and went downstairs to make coffee and wait.

Penelope was fixing eggs when Steve arrived. He was with two other men who waited in the car in the alley.

"Come in," Homer said easily. "What's up?"

"They have no evidence. They aren't supposed to know about the prints or that they have pretty good evidence that someone is selling something from the hospital. They need Penelope to go back to work and appear normal. She doesn't have to snoop or do anything but what she ordinarily does, but she needs to be back there. There will be a couple of people who will watch out for her. She is in no danger, but you need to pack up and get back to Byford."

Homer said, "Damn."

"I don't blame you." Steve smiled. "Who lives here?"

"Cynthia. She's on a holiday."

"This carriage house is really something. What's upstairs? Homer, take me on a tour? I need a word in private."

Penelope complained, "You need to practice subtlety a lot more."

Steve smiled at her. But he and Homer went off up the stairs. It pleased Penelope that the sofa bed had been slept in, too. That would give Steve something to think about. Then she remembered that she and Homer had gotten out on opposite sides of the bed, and the covers would show that. Oh, well.

Upstairs, Steve looked around and said, "This is really neat. Who is Cynthia? This a picture of her?"

"Yes. Penelope took that of Cynthia."

Steve whistled softly. "I need an introduction."

"We'll arrange it."

"You say she's on vacation? When's she due back?"

"Early May, if I recall her note. I don't want Penelope back at that place alone."

"There's no problem. The people at the hospital don't know that the police know anything."

"They did a strip search on her and a police officer."

"Stupid," Steve agreed. "But they believe they're in control and that the police think they were protecting the dope head. Penelope will be all right. The Byford chief wouldn't ask her to go back if he wasn't sure of that."

"I thought we were supposed to stay here until it was all over. I was supposed to be her protection. Now you say that you're going to remove me from her and send her out alone."

"It's your chief," protested Steve. "Not me."

"I don't like this one damned bit."

"There's no problem. Of course, if I were you and had this setup and Penelope, and I was told it was over before it'd barely begun, I'd be mad as hell, too. Just like you."

"I don't believe it's safe for her to go out there without me." Homer was terse.

"They can't figure a reason for you to go with her. She has to go alone. They want it all to be as normal as possible so that the people that have been put in there are safe and free to find out what's going on. You have to recognize that."

"I do. I just don't like it."

"You need to get her back there by nine-thirty at the very latest. You'll need to leave here not later than eight. It's now almost seven. Better get going."

"Damn." Homer's teeth gritted.

"Yeah."

They went back downstairs, and Penelope had breakfast ready. Steve was apologetic but declined, winked at Homer and went off, saying, "The guys in the alley would kill me if I sat in here enjoying your company and eating. Mostly the eating, since they haven't seen Penelope. You two take care of yourselves. Let me know how this all comes out."

And he left.

Nine

We have less than an hour," Homer said pensively.

Penelope was organized. "I'll do the kitchen, you strip the beds. We have to get some things washed and in the dryer."

He blinked. "I thought we'd make love."

She turned and looked at him, then she almost smiled. "You have a one-track mind."

"I don't want you to go out there to the hospital by yourself."

"They have no reason to fear me."

He opened his mouth to say—

"I know. The strip search. But Homer, there are a lot of good people who work out there, and most of them like me. Someone will be watching over me and—"

"They aren't there as your guards. They are there to find out what's going on. That's primary. You're a far second."

"And I can take care of myself."

He shut up. His worry could erode her self-confidence. "I want you to call me every two hours. I'll take you there and come get you when you're finished. Got that?"

"I might get busy and forget to call, and you'd get hyper."

He was offended. "Hyper?" Him?

"You tend to overreact."

"Not until I met you. You're like a loose cannon on the deck of a ship in rough seas. It's about impossible to get a handle on you."

"Loose cannon. That expression started with sailing ships? I'd just heard 'Loose cannon.' How long that expression has lasted! I can see why it's such a good illustration. Just think of—"

"And you tend to be distracted from the subject and go wandering off to other things."

She shrugged. "A fault."

He conceded, "You don't have too many."

"Why, thank you." She smiled at him, then her expression became pensive. "This was going to be such a thrilling time. I hate going away from here. It's been ideal."

"You are."

"Other than a few minor faults? Like living with my parents and my wandering attention? I notice you've hung around talking until I finished clearing the kitchen. Need help stripping the beds?"

"Let's go up."

"Up? The stairs? A balloon?"

"I can see how you'd slowly drive a man crazy."

"With frustration? With a sense of inferiority? With—" She started up the stairs, and he followed.

"Why did your parents let you back in their house, once they'd gotten rid of you?"

"We're kin. They have a great sense of kinship."

"That might account for it." He stopped her at the top of the stairs. "Penna-lope. Make love with me."

"How can you even *possibly* consider expending all that energy when we still have so much to do here?"

"Let me love you."

"Again. Add that. You've made love to me twice in less than twelve hours. That has to be a record of some sort."

"Kiss me."

As he held her to him, she folded her arms on his chest and propped her chin on top of her forearms, looking up at him. "A kiss would be a foot in the door."

He shook his head, grinning, and kissed her. And it was a foot in the door. He laid her on the sofa bed and made efficient love to her, taking a total of seventeen minutes, fourteen of which he used dallying, waiting for her to get excited enough.

She found it interesting that he got up, straightened his clothing and began to strip the bed. "Why did you go to sleep after the first two times, and not now?"

"No time. Hustle up."

"If it isn't one thing, it's another."

"Come on, woman. Hop."

"Hop! I can barely move!"

"Here, take my hand."

"I have learned, in these last few hours, that touching you is an invitation to an exhausting wrestling match."

He sat down beside her and smoothed her hair back from her face. "Have I exhausted you? God, Pennalope, you are so...magic. I can't—"

"I am almost living proof that you most certainly can!" She got up and scuttled across the sofa bed to the other side, escaping.

But he was serious. "Honey—"

"Let's strip this bed. You can take the sheets down and put them in the washer while I shower—again. I'll make up the bed while you're showering, then we can dry one load and wash the next—Cynthia's clothes I've worn, the dish towels, the bath towels. Then we should be ready to leave."

He watched her for a long minute, and she returned his gaze soberly, sadly. He said "Yes" in a very positive way. The word could be interpreted any number of ways. But he seemed satisfied with whatever he'd found in his version.

Hampering their preparations in leaving was one interruption. On the window frames, the windows swung inward on one side and the screens swung outward on the other. Very convenient. So Penelope pulled open the window, pushed open the screen and shook the Holland cover out over the alley.

In two minutes there was a man in the house! Homer was in the shower, and Penelope screamed as the stranger came charging up the stairs. Homer came dashing, naked, from the shower, and the intruder yelled, "What's going on?" in excited anger. And he added, "Tell her to quit that." And he repeated,

"What's going on? Why did you wave that sheet out the window?"

It was one of their guardians. Homer calmed him down, then they placated a furiously indignant Penelope, during which the distracted woman went to the wall and took down one of the Balinese ornamental fans and handed it to the naked Homer.

Then things got a little out of hand, and the guardian nobly tried not to laugh.

After the guardian left, Homer regarded Penelope thoughtfully and asked, "What's the top price your parents have offered for you to move out again?"

She gave him a stifling look and went back to finish the bed.

Standing there naked and dripping on the rug, he watched her. Then he went back to the shower.

Penelope wrote a note to Cynthia as had been requested: "You'd never believe all this. I'll be in touch. Thanks for a haven. Love, Penelope." That ensured Cynthia's getting in touch the day she returned.

Homer helped as Penelope finished tidying the carriage house. Inevitably they stood silently and looked at it from the front door, then went out, locked the door and put the key away. As they took their few possessions to the garage, Homer couldn't resist a delayed comment, "And you call me hyper."

She retorted parsimoniously, "Until I met you, my life was ordered and serene. Never before in all my memory has a man come charging up any of the stairs with a drawn gun."

He nodded thoughtfully. "That would catch your attention the first time."

"First time!" she exclaimed. "How many times have you seen that?"

"Several."

"And you can now take it in stride?"

"Well...no. But if it's done by a 'friendly' who is unthreatening, and you can say something quick enough, it's generally okay."

"Generally." She dubiously tried out that word.

"Mostly."

They opened the two folding garage doors, and he backed the car into the alley. Penelope closed the doors and latched them. She turned around, and on impulse, waved one hand high around her head and called, "Thanks." Then she went and got into the car. But then, as Homer eased it along the uneven, bricked, alley surface, a man stepped out and gave a semiwave and smiled at them before he disappeared. It wasn't the one who'd charged up the stairs.

"There *were* more! I was being droll."

"We were very well watched. We even had the security of a Citizens Watch. Good neighborhood."

"Turn here and go two blocks up and then turn back. I want to show you where I went to the School of Fine Arts. Isn't this neighborhood marvelous? These are some of the first houses in Fort Wayne. See? And the river is just at the end of the street. There were so many places we could go to draw. Such a variety. It's perfect."

"So you and Cynthia met here?"

"Yes. But she stayed. I've always envied Cynthia that carriage house."

"If you could pry yourself away from your parents, you could get one for yourself."

"Carriage houses are like hens' teeth. And so many have been torn down. The bricks are old and soft.

Cynthia has a private income, so she has the means to preserve her place."

"She's a parasite," he judged as he drove on out to Highway 24. "I wouldn't touch her with a ten-foot pole."

"Solely to embarrass you, I will tell you the reason she isn't here: she's personally seeing to it that immunization serums are getting to where they need to go."

"Ouch." And saying that, his whole cell system remembered that was what Penelope had said when he'd first taken her. He looked over at her.

She gave him a quelling glance. "That'll teach you to swing your ten-foot pole so unthinkingly."

He grinned, trying not to, but he couldn't stop tightly smothered chuckles. She looked at him as if he were unfathomable, but how could he explain? As briefly intimate as they'd been, he didn't know her well enough to share that humor. Then he thought about his hunger for her. "Are you all right?"

"As in sane or as in comfortable?" she inquired.

"As in, did I exhaust you?"

"It must be the ultimate temptation. No wonder there are so many people in the world."

"How did you resist so long?" he wanted to know.

"I was raised very strictly, with an ingrained sense of responsibility."

"Why did you let me make love to you? When you offered Cynthia's carriage house, you must have known I would try."

She shrugged. "I was never curious before this."

"I only made you . . . curious?" He was oddly offended.

"In these last seven or eight years, I've looked over a considerable segment of the male population, and I thought I might never marry. But I found that so much emphasis is placed on sex, that perhaps I ought to experience what I was giving up."

"Giving up?" He was appalled.

"Yes. If I don't marry, I see no reason to . . . be involved with some man."

"So you're giving up on marriage?"

"Well, I may look a little harder," she admitted.

"You liked it . . . with me?"

"You must have had a good deal of experience."

"Not that much." He shook his head slowly. "You are the temptation. I wanted you the first time I saw you."

"You opened that door, and I had to look at you closely. I felt I already knew you."

"Yes." He smiled just a bit.

"I figured out that you remind me of a roughneck that I knew in civics class in high school."

"A roughneck?" He frowned.

"You are more polished. You could go anywhere. That guy stuck out like a sore thumb just in class. He was quiet, courteous, and looked like he was in a fight before and after school. He was always healing or in slings. I suppose, now, that he was a battered child. I have no idea. He never had his homework done. The teachers were kind to him but frustrated. He looked as if he could handle anything. He joined the marines as soon as he could, and I have no idea what happened to him."

"So. You think I look as if I can handle things?" He invited her to flatter him.

"No question. I've seen you do it."

"I haven't handled anyone that you've seen."

"Me."

"You like the way I handled you?" He smiled again.

"You gave me courage when we left the hospital with the negative copies. You were so confident. I was impressed."

He was disappointed. He wanted her to talk about making love with him. He wanted to hear sweet words from her.

She had dismissed the subject. "It doesn't take long to get to Byford when we drive straight there. I'd never seen the roads or the countryside we took to get to Fort Wayne yesterday. Was it just...yesterday? So much has happened."

"Are you sorry?" Again he sought to talk about their lovemaking.

"No, they need to be exposed. You are right." While she did say that, her reluctance was still there. "There has to be some snakes' nest in that hospital. I was an inadvertent part of the exposé, but I'm glad it happened. I had nothing to do with the doctor's decision. He'd already made up his mind. And he wanted to be caught or he, too, would have closed the door. That's odd. I hadn't thought of that. He wanted to be caught." She considered that for a minute. "But I would swear that he didn't know I had taken those several pictures of him through the door. I was attracted by the dawn in the background and his pensive mood. It was a brilliant composition into which any number of things could be read at will, depending on the mood of the viewer. Speaking of wanting to be caught, do you suppose the maintenance couple like the risk of sneaking sex, and the possibility of being caught lends a feeling of excitement to the clandestine coupling?''

"Possibly."

"The fact that they hadn't closed the door has stymied me. It was such a simple solution. That they might want to be seen has to be a part of the explanation. They are closet exhibitionists, which is contradictory."

"Your mind goes a mile a minute." He grinned.

"It entertains me."

"I think you ought to get a job with the police department as a crime photographer. I could put in a recommendation for you."

"Thanks, but I'm entrenched at the hospital. I hope it survives whatever is happening out there. I hope the scandal is contained. I hope it isn't someone I like."

"I'd put good money on Kilroy." Homer's eyes narrowed. "There's something oily about him."

"Well, that lets him out. It's always the butler—you know that. It's never anyone obvious. Kilroy is probably as alerted as you are and is doing a shakedown, right now, finding out what's going on and who's responsible."

Homer was sure. "I'll bet you lunch at Amy's that it all turns on Kilroy. He's the kingpin."

"You're still mad about the strip search."

"It galled me. That pip-squeak."

"Pip-squeak?" The word surprised her.

"That was a last-minute word substitution. I have an uncle who uses that label with a pronunciation that leaves no doubt about exactly what he means."

"You do very well, saying it."

"You should hear my uncle."

There was a brief silence, then she said quietly,
"We're almost there."

"We have to drop the car off at Mary's first."

"What's Mary's real name?"

He explained: "Whoever is there, is called Mary. It
simplifies things."

"Who was Mary Ferris?"

"She owned the house originally. She liked cops.
We made her an honorary member. She 'watched.' She
was responsible for our first big drug bust. She saw a
neighborhood trash can carried out, then noticed that
people would come along the alley and open only that
can, take something out, but then they put something
in. She told us. We used her house as a stakeout. She
fed us the entire time and was very interested. So when
she died, she gave us the house. We named it Mary
Ferris, and that way it's still hers. Don't ever talk
about it. That's a rule."

He backed into the last driveway they'd used in Byford and into that garage. Then they got out and
walked across the alley to Mary Ferris's garage and on
into the house. Mary greeted them with apparently no
curiosity. He wasn't any cleaner. He flicked a thumb
over to the tiny bedroom and said, "The clothes are in
there."

So they went in and changed into cops' uniforms.
Then, leaving the clothing they'd worn from there,
they went out, got into a squad car and drove back to
police headquarters. Penelope changed into her original clothes, and still in uniform, Homer drove Penelope out to the hospital.

"May I call my family? How much can I say?"

"Say you're back in town, at work, and you'll explain later."

"If . . . I should need you, how do I find you?"

"Call the police number and when it rings twice, punch two. That's me. I'll be there all day and all night if I need to be. Penna-lope . . . be careful. Be suspicious. Don't go anywhere with anyone, no matter what the circumstances. Understand? If there's a fire drill, be sure you're with a bunch of people. Don't be alone." He pulled the car over to the curb and turned to hold her arms so that he could drill his stare back into the very depths of her eyes and therefore engrave it on her brain. "Don't trust nobody. Got that?"

Then he groaned and held her tightly. He finally allowed her some air and peered into her face in some agitation. "Watch yourself. Be alert to danger. Guard yourself."

"Got it."

He frowned down at her. She smiled. He added, "Take this seriously."

"Nothing could possibly happen to me in that place."

"Don't leave it until I come for you at five. Understand?"

She was patient. "I'm a quick study. Your instructions are redundant."

He sat back under the wheel and put his fists on it as he looked up at the sky and breathed heatedly, "Good God Almighty."

"Hyper," she judged, and looked out the car window. Then she looked at her watch and said, "If you don't hurry, I'll be late."

"You have on the same clothes you wore yesterday. People will remember that."

"I have on a coat. I have two other blouses at work. No problem."

"Green ones." That was to show her he was observant.

"As a matter of fact, one is green."

"What's the other one?"

"Purple."

"Wear it."

"Why?"

"Not many people wear purple, and that way I can find you easier."

"Okay. I grant your request."

She was not acting like a woman. She was acting like a man—stupid and easy. He drew in a deep breath to blast and rattle her, and his training again kicked in to remind him that she needed confidence. She didn't need to be scared and jumping at any sound. She needed to feel she could cope—alone if she must. He mentally bowed to equal rights, knowing he'd be there if it was necessary. She didn't have to realize how much danger there was. He demanded, "Kiss me."

She did that sweetly. Then she put one small hand to the side of his head and comforted him. "Don't worry so. It will be all right."

Steam should have shot out of his ears. He saw red. But he was disciplined. He released her, set her back on her side of the seat, then he put the car into gear, looked out for approaching traffic and drove sedately to the hospital.

If ever Homer had needed it, Penelope Rutherford had convinced him that women had no place in his life. They were too strange a breed. He had enough to think about and solve without the complications of a woman. He would reject her.

He drove along silently, trying to remember when she'd begged for his attention. She never had. Had she even just *invited* his attention? No, she hadn't. It had been his idea all along. Of course, she had suggested Cynthia's hideaway. She had done that. And she hadn't made up the sofa bed until she got mad at him. She had planned to lure him into her bed. She had. He faced it: because she was . . . curious.

He sent a scathing look over at the Medusa sitting alongside him with her snakelike writhing hair enclosed innocently in a large, soft, green tam. He'd made a lucky escape. His sense of duty and protection had almost entrapped him with a woman who would have driven him right up the wall . . . after her . . . scrabbling with his fingernails and toenails, trying to get to her. He sighed in self-pity.

She didn't even ask him what was the matter. Any woman hearing him sigh that way would know that he was troubled, but she just looked out the car window as if they were on a pleasant ride. "Tell me the police number and how to get me."

She repeated it obediently.

The car slowed as they approached the hospital. He wasn't aware of it, but Penelope was. It touched her how reluctant he was to let her out of his care. He was a darling man. He needed some good woman. She tried to think of one who would suit him better than she, who wouldn't anger him so, who would be more submissive. She could think of some wishy-washy women, but none was suitable.

He was going five miles per hour as they crept through the parking lot. She wanted to laugh, but she didn't want to offend him. She needed to have nothing more to do with him. She needed to guard herself against the violently wild feelings he caused to riot inside her.

Needlessly he said, "We're here."

"Thank you for everything."

He waited.

She moved to leave the car. He got out, adjusting his billy club automatically. He looked around, moving as do all wrestlers, football players, marines and cops. When he opened the door for her, she realized he planned to escort her all the way upstairs to her office. "Don't come in," she said. "You'll call attention to me."

She was right. "Call me."

She shook hands with him. "Thank you."

"Call me." His voice urged her.

"If I need you."

"Call me at eleven to tell me you're all right."

She smiled tenderly. "Hyper."

And his voicebox said, "Yeah." She laughed and the sound danced through his body.

Effortlessly she went on through the heavy doors, and he stood watching her but she didn't look back.

Disgruntled, he went to the squad car, got in and drove skillfully back to the station, using his siren to avoid two red lights. She might need to call him right away. She might find that nest of vipers in her office when she got there. A chill went up his back.

And she did. She opened her door, and there was Dr. Kilroy. He was there. He rose from her desk and smiled. It was an oily smile, just as Homer had labeled it. She smiled back. "You're here early."

She didn't removed her coat but stood, waiting to be told why he was there. "Something you need?"

"We have the negatives. They were in the woman's rest room. We need the rest of them printed. Would you do that this morning? We wonder if any of the prints might be the cause of the theft of your camera.''

"I'll do it right away."

"Thank you, my dear. I knew I could depend on you. Where were you last night? I called your home. Your father said you weren't there." Behind his glasses his oily eyes inspected her coated body as if she was naked. That surprised her, and she automatically crossed her arms in the feminine barrier.

She stepped back as if making way for him, and gestured to the open door as she said, "I'll deliver them as soon as they are finished? Or shall I bring down each segment?"

Dr. Kilroy said, "I thought I'd watch."

"You're welcome to do that. I need about a half hour to get organized. Would you like to come back, then? Let me get you a smock. The chemicals can stain some materials. Take it with you and put it on. This one is clean."

"Do I strip?" Kilroy's voice was almost playful.

She didn't look at him. How dare he remind her that she'd been strip searched. Was he trying to make a sexual joke of it? She said firmly, "When I call, remove your suit coat and roll up your shirtsleeves, then put on the smock."

"What are you going to do now?"

She reported perfunctorily, "Sort the mail and go get the proper grade of paper for the prints."

"Forget the mail. Just call Supply. I'll tell them to deliver it."

"I prefer to do it personally. In Supply, they are very busy. I always go get the materials myself."

"Today can be the exception," he said silkily.

"They will think it odd. If you want to keep any investigation under control and quiet until you know if there is anything going on, then the routine should stay the same. You really ought not take this time to watch the printing. Satisfy your curiosity another time. If you are watching me print after the camera was returned, someone will know you are curious. And they will wonder why. You might precipitate something you're not yet ready to handle." Her face was expressionless.

"You do have a point." He paced a bit in her tiny office, and she stayed carefully out of the way so that he couldn't brush against her. He decided, "Bring down the segments as you get them printed. You have to know how curious we are about these prints."

She shook her head. "I doubt if there will be anything. If you found the negatives discarded, they must be okay."

"I'll send one of the security men to sit in your office and accompany you to my office. Be careful."

But Penelope noted that he wasn't at all alarmed.

Ten

Dr. Kilroy assured Penelope that he would be waiting for the prints of the first segment of her film. She nodded formally, not smiling. She closed the door after him and went into her darkroom. It had been riffled. Nothing was far out of line, but she knew someone had been through everything in that room.

She changed into the purple blouse and put on a smock, pinning it high to her throat. Not having a safety pin, she used the enameled green-moth pin that Homer had given her, and which she carried in her purse. Then she went needlessly down to Supply and drew enough paper of the grade to make reasonable prints of the film. And on the way back, she ducked into an empty office and dialed Homer.

His voice said, "Yeah?"

"Standing by?" She had reversed his code.

"Ready," he replied tersely.

"Stand by."

She put down the phone and escaped undetected. It had been cruel to alert Homer in that way. But no names had been used. It hadn't been her phone. She had piffled all Homer's warnings, and the Pit Bull needed to know that she was now uneasy.

She went upstairs and chose which segment she should do first. She chose the student nurse. As they were drying, she did the maintenance couple. Those should distract Kilroy. Would he see the truth about them as easily and quickly as Homer? From the manner in which Kilroy had looked at her, she thought he would. How strange that she'd worked there for two years and not attracted his attention before this.

While that segment of prints was drying, Penelope took the student's pictures to Dr. Kilroy. The prints were in an envelope and she simply handed it to Dr. Kilroy's secretary and said, "He is waiting for these."

"Thanks, Penny. I'll take them in right away."

Penelope went up the stairwell thoughtfully, wondering if the student would be discharged. She felt some regret. Surely a student would only be disciplined. Then Penelope comforted herself that someone had been supervising the student, and on those shoulders rested the responsibility.

No one learned everything right away, and she remembered herself as a student and her first botched batch of film. She still mourned a couple of irreplaceable pictures in that bunch. A hard lesson; but she'd never lost another.

She decided to risk calling Homer, the Pit Bull, and tell him what was going on. But when she reached her floor and walked into her office, there was Dr. Kilroy, waiting, in smock. Now she had another problem.

She looked more surprised than she was and said, "I just delivered the first batch down to you."

"May I go in? I didn't want to ruin anything that might be in progress."

"I'll call Maggie."

"Why?"

"Rules," she reminded him. "Your reputation."

"I trust you, Penelope."

"The administrative head is especially vulnerable to scandal. I'll call Maggie from staff." And busily efficient, she picked up the phone and dialed. Since her section was separate from the general offices, in that mishmash of buildings, Penelope would have to dial several numbers. With each series, she would ring through to another patch until finally she would punch in Maggie's number. If Kilroy had been watching her fingers' movements, he would have known she had dialed outside. She had called the Pit Bull. She said, "Dr. Kilroy would like to witness the printing of the photographs. Could you come in?"

"Standing by."

"Oh, I beg your pardon." She hung up and explained, "Wrong number." She redialed and said again, "Dr. Kilroy would like to witness the printing of some photographs. Could you come in?" She was unaware she'd changed a word. Instead of "the" photographs, she'd said "some" photographs.

Maggie replied, "Sure, Penny. Two minutes."

But Dr. Kilroy then said, "I especially want to see those taken from the roof. How much of the operation can you see?"

"It was for a panorama effect. From inside, each operation is isolated. This allowed seeing the whole series of rooms. And I caught a marvelously beautiful angle along the roofline that is spectacular."

"How do you know that?"

"I developed the film."

"Then you've seen only that film?"

"Of course. Except for the pictures you already have of Dr. Stanton."

A man tapped on the door, and Penelope turned sharply, expecting to be glad to see the Pit Bull. It was only a maintenance man. He said, "Someone complained about flickering lights and I have to check the fuses and connections." He came into the room with a large toolbox and an awkward ladder.

"Now?" Kilroy asked impatiently.

"Yeah. With all the ethers and sprays, flickering lights can give off sparks and *Boom!*" he explained placidly.

So Dr. Kilroy told Penelope sourly, "Never mind, I really don't have the time. We'll do it another day. Cancel Maggie. Bring the next batch down when they're ready. Do the roof ones and you can show me the line you find so exciting." He looked down her body again before he left.

She couldn't prevent a small back-shoulder shiver of distaste, and she closed the door rather firmly.

A quiet soft voice said, "A real bastard."

"You know Dr. Kilroy?" Penelope inquired.

"Just met him for the first time."

"Be careful. We might be bugged. He's vindictive."

"I've turned on a buzzer that'll negate any bug. I'm a cop. Name's Bob. I don't know a-a-a-anything about electricity except to try the switch, but I was the best Homer could get quick.''

''He is so sweet.'' Penelope smiled.

''Who?''

''Detective Homer.''

''He's...sweet?'' His tone was unbelieving.

''Yes.''

''I'll be damned.''

''Didn't your mother ever wash out your mouth with soap?''

''Not after I got bigger'n her. And that was young. She's only about four-eleven.''

''She should have worn stilts,'' Penelope judged.

Bob laughed. ''Since there's nothing wrong with the electricity, is there anything I can do to help you with the pictures?''

''You know about the pictures?''

''I'm the police photographer that Homer's trying to push aside...for you.''

''How rude of him.'' Penelope was a little smug.

''Now, *rude* sounds like Homer. Are you finished with the couple? That was brilliant photography. She's probably thirty-five, anyway. That's a little old for me, but I'll bet she's tasty. Seeing those pictures would set any man afire.''

Penelope was shocked. ''A...fire?''

''Yeah, you know what they've been doing, and it's enflaming.'' Bob grinned.

''Good grief.''

''Get used to me, we're twins until Homer can figure a way to get to you himself. But don't get excited about me. You can't have my body. On duty, I'm pure.''

She laughed. And she felt safe. The Pit Bull was watching out for her, utilizing this nut. And she thought tenderly of Homer's frustration in not being there himself.

But he was. He was just then establishing a beachhead in the stairwell, washing walls. It was the only centrally located spot that he could be and not attract attention, and washing walls was it. He did a good job. He was mad and had excess energy.

So when she carried down the maintenance couple's pictures, he straightened and said, "Lady..."

She dropped the pictures and got nervous and melting and very disorganized. Almost instantly, he saw the green moth pin, and he kissed her there on the stairs again, even though that was a dangerous place to do anything so disorienting. So she floated the rest of the way down the stairs and arrived at Kilroy's office looking...different.

She looked like some man had just kissed her. Her eyes were smug, her lips a little puffed, and her hair looked excited, curling and straying from neatness.

Kilroy's secretary said, "He wants you to come in right away."

Penelope replied, "I can't. I left some of the prints in the bath and I've got to get back."

But she lingered on the stairs. Since *any* sound carried in that stairwell, they whispered in each other's ear and he kissed her some more. She told him, "He wants me to personally give him the roof ones."

And Homer whispered back, "Let me figure it out."

"He's shown great interest in my body today, even with my coat on."

The Pit Bull frowned, really mean-looking.

"Why don't you just arrest him?"

"For what?" he asked her.

"Oh."

Someone came into the stairwell and started up. Homer released Penelope and she wavered. He steadied her, and she wobbled on up the stairs on those damned high heels of hers.

So later when she came down very slowly, waiting for a lull in stairwell traffic, she was carrying the roof pictures. Homer said, "Reverse the sequence of the roof pictures."

"I can't. The operational procedures are exact."

"Damn."

That was all the time they had, because the stairwell was so busy then with converging traffic. Homer whispered into a little mike, "Bob, stairwell, on the double." Then he said singularly: "Entrances. Cars."

Penelope dreaded having to be in the same room with Dr. Kilroy—even briefly. The secretary waved her on by, and Penelope went into the office with the envelope. She greeted Murgurd. That was unsettling. Why was he there with Kilroy?

She handed the envelope across the desk to Kilroy and said, "That's just about all of them." She noted the other pictures were back in their carrying envelopes. Kilroy didn't look her over this time, but slid the pictures out of their envelope and spread them on the desk. Murgurd went over to look at them.

Aware it was an opportunity, Penelope quietly turned and walked to the door, opened it...and it was shut as she was pulled back! Murgurd. She managed to look surprised and asked, "What?" And she frowned at him, lifting her arm to indicate he was to let go. Murgurd smiled.

"Let go," she said, enunciating clearly.

He replied heartily with a streak of meanness, "Come over here and let's look at the pictures."

Kilroy said, "Yes. You are a very skilled photographer. These pictures show everything."

She looked interested as she moved back to the desk. "Too much? I thought the divisions in the windowpanes covered the patients enough. As I told you, it was for the panoramic effect. Look at that."

"And this roofline is the one that you're proud about?" Dr. Kilroy ran his oily finger along it.

"It's a perfect balance for the straight lines of the windows and bricks. A good strong line."

"And this truck?" Murgurd pointed to it.

"See how perfectly it balances that long slanted line? And it carries the straight line of the windows. Such miraculous happenstance. To have it be unloading at that time was such pure luck." She might as well admit the damned truck was there and to pretend it was unloading.

"Un-loading." Dr. Kilroy tested the word.

"The boxes, for the kitchen . . . she explained.

"Yes," said Kilroy thoughtfully. "Unloading." He sat back in his chair and looked at Murgurd. Murgurd grinned.

Penelope began to breathe again. "I have only about five more to print, and there are three in the bath. I have to get back."

"Yes." Kilroy came around his desk and took her arm, escorting her to the door. "You do a fine job here. We all appreciate you."

"Thank you." She opened the door and—there stood the Pit Bull! He looked thunderous, and he was disguised in Maintenance clothing. It was a dead giveaway.

Everything went sour.

Kilroy jerked her back inside and slammed the door. He snarled at Murgurd, "How'd Homer get Maintenance coveralls?"

Murgurd drew his gun. For just a minute, Penelope thought he was going to make Kilroy let her go, but he said, "I don't know, but I'll sure as hell find out."

"If he's out there in Maintenance clothes, it's hit the fan." Then Kilroy looked at Penelope. "Who was that guy who came into your office? Another cop?"

"Cop?"

Kilroy clutched her hair and shook her head. She knew that if she screamed, Homer would break down the door and Murgurd would shoot him.

"Kilroy!" yelled Homer. "What's going on in there?"

Murgurd said calmly, "Look. The place is surrounded."

And Kilroy whined, "No-o-o." And he pulled Penelope's hair, waggling her head. She made a sound as she drew in a tortured breath.

Murgurd looked surprised, then said in disgust, "What are you doing? You fool. She's our ticket out of here."

Kilroy straightened. "Out of here?"

"My God, you're stupid! I thought you had control. You're really dumb. Get yourself together. You have to keep yourself organized and watch yourself if we're to get away. What are you doing?"

"The money."

"Shut up," Murgurd warned. "We've got enough. Don't get too greedy, it might kill you."

Kilroy straightened and became harsh-faced. He said, "You're right. We'll take her along." He looked down Penelope. "I always wondered what you'd be like. Now we'll know, won't we."

Stunned by the thought, she said, "Good God. You are incredible."

"Yes."

Murgurd told him, "She was insulting you. Get hold of yourself. You're coming undone. Give me the girl. You're going to mess it up."

"No! She's mine! Give me my gun."

Penelope could only think: loose cannon. And her knees weakened. Then the things that happened became slow and segregated. Murgurd gave Kilroy his gun from a drawer in the desk. The prints of the roof pictures slid onto the floor. From behind her, Kilroy put an arm hurtfully around her chest, squashing her breasts with his forearm. She reached up a hand to pull his arm down, and her fingers encountered the green moth pin. Homer.

Murgurd yelled through the door, "Get away from the door. No need to tell you that we have the girl. Tell the rest to get away and let us go, or...she...dies."

It was all ridiculous. Penelope had seen this same scene how many times on television or in films? It was so dumb. It was unreal. She heard Homer say "Okay. Wait a minute. I've got to tell everybody. Don't get nervous. It's all right. Nothing's going to happen. Just be calm." Penelope wondered how much of that soothing talk was for her? Kilroy was a loose cannon. A loose cannon had to be lashed down. Who got the job? Did they expect her to do it? How?

The door was opened. Homer's voice was steady, and from him flowed an unbroken stream of reassurance. Nothing was going to happen. Walk carefully. Don't trip. Steady. All the calming words.

They edged through the door, very much like a six-legged spider. Murgurd was afraid they would pick him off, so he was close. Dr. Kilroy's secretary was back against the wall like a pinned butterfly looking on in fascinated horror.

It was a dream. A nightmare. But Homer's voice was the link to sanity.

Weaponless, he walked sideways in front of them, watching them like a hungry buzzard, a Pit Bull. He was half crouched. His voice never betrayed his tension. He was magnificent.

The trio of fleeing people edged along toward the back entrance that led to the parking lot. As they approached the door, Homer changed tactics. "Kilroy, what did you do? Why are you doing this? Why do you feel you have to run? Is someone threatening you?"

Murgurd said, "Shut up."

"Shoot him!" Kilroy commanded.

Murgurd retorted, "Don't be any more stupid than you are now."

Homer's voice went on: "Be careful you don't trip. Watch yourselves on the stairs. You have nothing to fear from us. We'll see to it that you get away from here. Be careful now, of the stairs. I don't want her hurt."

As they reached the first step, the six-legged entity groped and got down it. And Homer's calming voice said, "Two more. Don't trip." Then came the second step.

As their awkward mass negotiated it, Penelope put her right foot behind her left knee and kept it there,

and she plunged the green moth enameled pin into
Kilroy's arm.

They began to fall, and instinct made them all react
differently. But Kilroy pulled his arm up in shock, and
Penelope said a soft "Ouch!"

That triggered Homer, the Pit Bull, and he leaped
into the mass. Guns went off, and the shocks of the
loud sounds reverberated deafeningly in that con-
fined space. There were yells: "Get 'em! Get 'em!"
And savage, nonword sounds from men's throats. A
melee ensued, with wresting and wrestling. And it was
over.

But at the bottom of the steps lay a silent Penelope.
Homer stood in suspended terror and looked down on
her. His head was forward. He was dressed in those
green coveralls and heavy shoes. His body was so
primitively male. He leaned slowly down as if straining to move in a clear, solid mass. It seemed his hands
would never reach her.

He squatted and reached and touched her. She
moved and said again, "Ouch." She was alive.

There was certainly enough medical help. The fallen
ones were quickly assessed. The fake electrician, Bob,
was one who was down. He had been shot through the
stomach by Murgurd. He writhed, his teeth gritted.
Murgurd had a bloodily smashed hand. Kilroy was
untouched except for the broken jaw Homer had provided. And the Pit Bull was leaking red stuff that
splatted down on the tile in large drops.

A doctor said to Homer, "Lie down."

"Help her."

"She's okay. She just hit her head, and she's
scared."

"Is she all right?"

The doctor nodded. "As soon as she realizes it, she'll be okay. You're hurt."

"I'm okay."

"You're leaking blood."

Penelope stirred but her eyes didn't open. Her pale lips said, "Where's the Pit Bull?"

The doctor frowned at her. "Maybe she hit harder than I thought."

"She wants me," Homer explained.

"Pit Bull?" The doctor raised his eyebrows.

"Yeah."

The doctor laughed. "Lie down."

"Homer?" she asked, her eyes still closed. "Are you okay?"

"Yeah," her love replied.

"You're alive?" she urged.

"Yeah."

"Good." She fainted.

"My God!" Homer was frantic. Tears started in his eyes.

"She just fainted," the doctor soothed. "She's been through quite a bit, she deserves a faint."

"You're sure she's all right."

"On my honor. Here, lie down."

"I feel . . . odd," Homer mentioned.

"I'm not surprised."

Homer always wore his badge, and he had it on his undershirt under the coveralls. He said, "You never know when you're going to have to prove which side you're on." So the bullet had hit that and slid off it, plowed along under his skin and exited off his hip. It was painful but not serious. He was kept at the hospital for a while. He would have to get a new badge.

Bob had been taken immediately to surgery and wasn't horrifically damaged by the bullet. Bad enough. But he was healthy and young, and he came along nicely.

And Penelope stayed for two days under observation. She had a badly bruised knee that was very painful.

Someone had videotaped the whole proceedings from the opening of Kilroy's door, and sold the film to CNN, and Penelope's little sister had taped it from the TV report. Mrs. Rutherford hadn't seen it . . . and couldn't. But her sister told Penelope, "Wait 'til you see Homer! He was a hero!"

The Pit Bull.

On the second day, Penelope's parents and family arrived with copies of the paper. "We were here earlier and got to look at you to reassure ourselves. You might have told us what was going on. It's a surprise when someone comes to our door and mentions we might like to see our daughter who has been in a gunfight."

"They couldn't have been that blunt," Penelope demurred.

"They weren't," her dad assured her.

"I'm sorry about—"

"We understand." Her dad took her hand. "Homer is okay. You do know that? He'd like to see you, and they won't let him up yet."

"I'm going after visiting hours." Penelope sighed. "His family is there now."

Then Winslow's mother and father came in and introduced themselves, and they were all awkward in a friendly way as they eyed each other and wondered about the other family.

When visiting hours were over, a nurse came in with a wheelchair and said Penelope could go see the hero—and she had better, because all the nurses were finding excuses to go see him.

"I can walk," Penelope informed the nurse.

"We'd rather you didn't until tomorrow."

"I'm really okay." Penelope was firm.

"Let's do it our way." The nurse smiled.

Penelope took a deep breath and said sweetly, "Of course."

"Good attitude. Everything is easier for a patient who has a good attitude."

Penelope finished it: "And does everything your way."

"Right."

"How spineless."

"Thank God you won't be here long." The nurse heaved a sigh. "You'd be a . . . challenge."

"You'll get that from the Pit Bull."

The nurse looked the question.

"Winslow Homer."

The nurse laughed. "You've pegged him."

"Is he giving you trouble?"

The nurse gave Penelope a rueful look and nodded tiny nods.

"Figures."

The nurse warned Penelope: "He'll ask about Bob, so we'll take you for a quick look at him first, so you can tell the Pit Bull that Bob's okay. Okay?"

"Yes."

Bob was a little mellow. He smiled and smiled. Penelope told him, "Thank you, Bob."

"Any time. Did you know I was the one who got Murgurd? I got his hand. It was a brilliant shot."

"Yes," Penelope told him. "But I'm sorry you were hit."

"No big deal."

After they left Bob, Penelope asked the nurse, "What's he on?"

"A little painkiller. And he's so cute—and single— that everyone is spoiling him rotten."

A little stiffly, Penelope inquired, "And are they spoiling Winslow Homer?"

"Yes. But he doesn't soak it up like Bob. The Pit Bull is wild to get out of bed and get to Penelope Rutherford. He doesn't 'see' us as Bob does."

"I've been to see Homer," Penelope protested.

"He doesn't really remember it."

When Penelope was wheeled into his room, Homer's head turned sharply and he stared at her almost frantically. "Are you all right?"

"Yes. We're riding this chair because it's doing things their way."

Homer snarled. "Penna-lope. Don't lie to me. Are you all right?"

She turned to the nurse and said with intensity, "May I?"

The nurse locked the wheels and said, "You may." But she held Penelope's arm and was sure she didn't stumble.

What happened to the nurse after that, they never knew. Penelope limped slowly to the bed. Homer automatically tried to sit up, his arms held out longingly, but he gasped and lay back rigidly.

Penelope cried softly.

And Homer said, "Ouch."

"Oh, darling, are you all right?"

"Almost. Come around the other side."

She did that easily enough. And she lay beside him and petted his face and touched where she could and reassured them both. They kissed sweetly, but she wouldn't allow too many or too passionate kisses. "Not now," she whispered. And he groaned.

He said, "You were brilliant. You were so brave—"

"You were magnificent. So calm—"

"You understood about tripping. I was scared spitless."

"Did they find my pin? The one you gave me. The green moth, enameled one. I stuck it clear in his arm."

"So that's what you did. I thought you bit him. Have you seen Bob?"

Penelope nodded. "He's spaced-out and smiling and all the nurses are spoiling him rotten. He's funny. And he is okay."

"Weren't the guys great? For not knowing exactly what would happen, and each did exactly what he was supposed to, and in spite of the danger, they were all just great. I was impressed."

"Me, too. You were so calm."

"No." He denied it. "I was praying like blue blazes. God calmed my voice. The rest of me was on hold."

It was a week later when she gathered Homer's things and took him to his apartment. And she met the parrot. Homer was right—it didn't talk. It was stuffed.

Penelope said in an accusing way, "He's stuffed."

"I never said he wasn't. I just said he couldn't talk."

He had her green moth pin that one of the medics had hunted down. It was bent. "If you hadn't given me this pin, I wouldn't have had a weapon."

"It was tripping yourself that did it. You did a good job on that."

"It was the only way to discipline myself into falling. If I'd tried a pretend fall, it wouldn't have worked as well."

"You really needed to weigh about fifty more pounds to've done the job right. I never lived any nightmare to compare with seeing you unconscious on that floor. I love you, Penna-lope."

"And I love you." She was feeling mushy.

"Forever?"

"Yes. Do you think you can tolerate me and my quirks?"

"I'll try," he promised bravely. "You're an impossible woman. No submissive traits at all."

"Why didn't you just walk away from me?"

"I did try."

"Did you?"

"I couldn't."

She smiled. "I brought you a get-well present."

"You're that."

"I'll be right back."

"A cake?" he guessed, and watched her cross the room. "The bathroom? You're going to give us a bubble bath? I can't yet."

"Be quiet. This takes a lot of courage."

He waited, curious.

Finally she called through the door, "Are you ready?"

"I *think* so."

The bath door slowly opened, and he thought of another door opening in such danger and her coming through; but that was then and this was here and now. She emerged timidly, wearing an absolutely scandalous outfit from Frederick's of Hollywood. It wasn't much of anything, but it wasn't as red as her scarlet face.

"Why, Penelope Rutherford!"

"I won it some years ago playing bridge at a lingerie shower. I got top score."

"Scoring suits that outfit."

"Do I shock you?"

He licked his lips. "Come here."

"You're not nearsighted."

"Nearhanded," he explained logically.

"Oh."

"Yeah. Oh. Oh, Penna-lope, you are so beautiful. I love you."

"Do you?"

"Hell, honey, you have to know that by now."

"I wasn't sure. That's why I put on this outfit. I thought I could catch your attention."

"You've had it all along. You deliberately wore that long sweater to make me territorial, you have to admit that."

"Well, I did think I'd like to just . . . taste you."

"How did you like me?"

"I dusted off this outfit. It takes great motivation to actually wear something like this."

"Well, if it embarrasses you, take it off." His voice was husky.

She took a teasingly long time in unsuccessfully "trying" to remove the wisps. He groaned and reached, but she pushed his hands away and she laughed.

"You heartless woman. Come here to this poor wounded cop and make me well."

So she did. She went to him and told him that she loved him. She cuddled him carefully and put her hands into his clothes and touched him here and there, and teased and tormented and made him groan with his desire.

She allowed him to remove those silly red strings and gave him the freedom of her body. Then she encouraged him with sighs and tiny sounds that prickled along him, exciting him. And she helped him. She took his clothing away and laid him back, then she slid over him carefully and gave him surcease—slowly, deliciously and with great satisfaction.

They were married a scandalously short time after that. Cynthia came home in time for the wedding and the families had a big celebration. Cynthia said she had to take another batch of serum back, and if they would like to, they could stay awhile at her carriage house. And they did. And while they were there, Penelope developed the film that was taken of Homer as a painter, and she blew up the smug one and hung it on the wall.

They lay in bed and looked at it, and he grinned. But she said, "That's not an artist."

"No?"

"That's the sneaky Pit Bull pretending to be a lap-dog."

And Homer laughed out loud.

* * * * *

COMING NEXT MONTH

ANOTHER WHIRLWIND COURTSHIP
Barbara Boswell

Four years ago Chelsea Kincaid had walked away from domineering Cole Tremaine, and he'd never forgotten it — or forgiven her! Now Chelsea had jilted the President's son and needed somewhere to hide. Cole would help, but at a price!

THE HEART MENDER
Kathleen Creighton

Love was the last thing brokenhearted Jenna McBride thought she needed. But when she met a dangerous-looking biker called Reno she was mesmerized. She thought she would have a fling, but how do you control your heart?

FREE TO DREAM
Janet Franklin

An idle month in the Rockies would feel like an eternity to efficient Andrea MacLarson. Then broad-shouldered drifter Bart Collins entered her life, and every minute with him became time well spent!

COMING NEXT MONTH

JADE'S PASSION
Laura Taylor

Jade Howell had struggled to make her dream of a center for homeless children become a reality. There wasn't room in her life for a man — especially Reed Townsend, who had a secret that could tear them apart.

MAGGIE'S MAN
Jackie Merritt

Sloan Prescott had more on his mind than grazing rights when he thought of Maggie Holloway. He meant to keep his sheep on her land, but more importantly he meant to keep his boots under her bed — for good.

TWICE IN A BLUE MOON
Dixie Browning

Years before, January's *Man of the Month* Tucker Owen, had been the town's 'bad boy' — and loving Hope Outlaw, the preacher's daughter, had been an impossible dream. But that was then …

4 SILHOUETTE DESIRES
AND 2 FREE GIFTS
- yours absolutely free!

The emotional lives of mature, career-minded heroines blend with believable situations, and prove that there is more to love than mere romance. Please accept a lavish FREE offer of 4 books, a cuddly teddy and a special MYSTERY GIFT... Then, if you choose, go on to enjoy 6 more exciting Silhouette Desires, each month, at just £1.40 each. Send the coupon below at once to: Silhouette Reader Service, FREEPOST, PO Box 236, Croydon, Surrey CR9 9EL.

YES Please rush me my 4 Free Silhouette Desires and 2 Free Gifts! Please also reserve me a Reader Service Subscription. If I decide to subscribe I can look forward to receiving 6 brand new Silhouette Desires each month for just £8.40. Post and packing is free, and there's a Free monthly newsletter. If I choose not to subscribe I shall write to you within 10 days - but I am free to keep the books and gifts. I can cancel or suspend my subscription at any time. I an over 18. Please write in BLOCK CAPITALS.

Mrs/Miss/Ms/Mr _____ EP99SD

Address _____

_____

_____ Postcode _____
(Please don't forget to include your postcode).

Signature _____

The right is reserved to refuse an application and change the terms of this offer. Offer expires December 31st 1990. Readers in Southern Africa please write to P.O. Box 2125, Randburg, South Africa. Other Overseas and Eire, send for details. You may be mailed with other offers from Mills & Boon and other reputable companies as a result of this application. If you would prefer not to share in this opportunity, please tick box. ☐